NO FILTER

NO FILTER

KELLEY SKOVRON

SCHOLASTIC INC.

This book is a work of fiction. Names, characters, places, and incidents are either the product of the author's imagination or are used fictitiously, and any resemblance to actual persons, living or dead, business establishments, events, or locales is entirely coincidental.

ISBN 978-1-338-89316-8

10 9 8 7 6 5 4 3 2 1   24 25 26 27 28

First printing 2024

Printed in the U.S.A.   40

Book design by Stephanie Yang

FOR STEPHANIE

1

THE SMUDGE

It's ruined. Horribly, hideously ruined.

Janessa "Jinx" McCormick sits in front of her computer and glares at the image of strawberry ice cream on the monitor. She is twelve years old, with sharp green eyes and long straight blond hair parted down the middle. She wears her father's vintage black Nine Inch Nails *Pretty Hate Machine* T-shirt, which is much too big on her, and a pair of faded blue jeans that she has painstakingly shredded at the knees with a wire brush so they look like she bought them that way. She has a habit of biting her nails, and several fingers that she's nibbled to the quick are tipped with silver Band-Aids.

Jinx's computer rests on a mostly bare, white desk beneath the loft bed in her tiny six-by-eight bedroom. It's an odd Frankenstein PC that she and her friend Blaine cobbled together from spare parts. At the moment, she is using it to edit a photo from a shoot she took yesterday. The current picture wouldn't have been perfect no matter what. Maybe it could have been, if she was a professional photographer with a studio and a food stylist. But she isn't yet, and for the time being she'll live with the less-than-ideal lighting and the lackluster texture of the red strawberry chunks nestled into the pink ice cream.

What she *cannot* live with is the black smudge that has completely ruined the image. At a glance, it appears to be a fly perched on the ice cream. Obviously, that's not a great way to sell a food product. But she knows there was no fly when she took the shot. And when she zooms in, the smudge doesn't actually look like a fly. The trouble is, she can't tell *what* it is, and that's pretty weird.

Jinx shoots with a Canon 5D Mark III DSLR. Not the most cutting-edge camera out there now, but it *was* the best camera on the market a decade ago, and still has better control over ISO, aperture size, and shutter speed than even the best phone cameras. It also allows for a nearly infinite number of lens types that she could swap in and out to achieve various effects—assuming she could afford to buy them, which she can't. Regardless, while the camera is a bit old, it still takes really good pictures. So Jinx is able to zoom in incredibly close on the image. If it *had* been a fly, she would have been able to count the hairs on its legs. But even at that intense magnification, the black smudge is still . . . just a smudge.

Could it be something on her lens? She takes it out of the case that sits by her feet, holds it up, and examines it carefully. It's clean.

Of *course* it is, because she always wipes down her lens before packing it up. Even if there was a smudge during the shot, it was gone before she put it away.

While Jinx is still puzzling out the smudge mystery, her phone lights up. She prefers a clean workspace, so it's the only thing on her desk besides her computer. When she glances over, she sees a message from Blaine.

Jinxie! We still doing that shoot at the park?

She carefully wipes her lens and places it back in the case before answering.

Yeah see you in 20 min

Jinx looks back at the ice cream image. She could edit out the smudge, but it's only one photo in a whole set, and the rest are all smudge free. Besides, she promised Mr. Alsobrooks that she'd send him proofs today. So she deletes the image with the blemish, then exports the rest from RAW format to a smaller jpeg size and uploads those to her cloud service. She emails the share link to delvin@scream4icecream.com with a brief note:

Hi Mr. Alsobrooks. Let me know which one you like best and I'll send the full res —Jinx

Then she puts her computer on standby, grabs her camera bag, and heads downstairs.

Jinx lives in a two-bedroom town house with her aunt Helen. It's pretty small, but she doesn't mind because it means there's less space to clean. The downstairs is one big room, with a couch and TV in one area, and a small dinner table with four chairs in another. Off to one side is a kitchen that Jinx only really uses for making breakfast cereal. Occasionally, Aunt Helen will cook them a meal, but Jinx's aunt is a nurse who works the graveyard shift. Right now she's upstairs sleeping, and she probably won't wake up until about 5:00 p.m. That means Jinx's dinner time is usually her aunt's breakfast time. Not that Jinx needs someone to cook for her. She pretty much has the food situation under control.

She pauses at the front door to pull on her

black-and-white checkered high-top Vans, and grab her skateboard. When she's ready to leave the house, she rests her hand on the doorknob and taps a quick sequence on it with her bandaged fingertips:

Tappity-tappity. Tap. Tap. Tappity-tappity. Tap. Tap.

She nods in satisfaction, opens the door, and heads out into the world.

2

THE SKATER

Jinx has grown up her whole life in Greenbelt, Maryland. It was one of the first planned communities in America, built during the Great Depression as a way to spark growth and give people jobs. It's technically a city, but it's also the last stop on the Washington DC Metro, so a lot of people commute from Greenbelt to the nation's capital for work. Even Jinx goes to Smithsonian museums for her school field trips sometimes.

She usually stays in Greenbelt, though. It has pretty much anything she needs. She skates past Buddy Attick Park, which has a big man-made lake that was dug entirely by people with shovels. Not because they didn't have better tools back in the 1930s, but because it provided more jobs during a time when a lot of people were unemployed.

Past the park, she skates through the church parking lot and down a path next to a huge athletic field, with three baseball diamonds and several tennis courts. After all that, she reaches Roosevelt Center, which has the library, the city pool, a co-op grocery store, a few restaurants, a restored 1930s movie theater, and a community center. It also has a skate park, and that's where Jinx is meeting Blaine.

Jinx doesn't really consider herself a skater. She can't do many tricks and doesn't go to the park just to skate. For her, a skateboard is a convenient and portable means of travel. A bike would have worked just as well. Except they aren't quite as portable. Also, she doesn't have one.

The skate park is empty when she arrives. That's not surprising because it's pretty small compared to others in the area. It doesn't have any ramps, rails, or half-pipes. Just two cement bowls, one that's shallow for beginners, and one that's deeper for more experienced skaters. They look like empty, kidney-shaped swimming pools, since before official skate parks existed, that's what skaters used. The skate bowls are enclosed in a sturdy iron fence with several ALWAYS WEAR A HELMET signs fixed to it.

Of course Blaine isn't here yet. And she doesn't expect him for at least ten minutes, because he is never on time for anything. She's considered coming late herself sometimes, either to give him a taste of his own medicine or just so she doesn't have to wait as long. But she just . . . can't. Even if she's doing it on purpose and nobody else seems to care, being late stresses her out. It just feels *wrong*. So she always comes early, and he always comes late.

But at last he arrives. Blaine Chen has broad shoulders and black bangs that hang down from under the same faded purple Ravens cap that he's had for as long as Jinx can remember. He's about four years older than her and already in high school. They used to be neighbors back when Jinx lived with her father, and he's always been sort of a big brother to her. Sometimes he still treats her like a little kid, but it's nice to know that he's always looking out for her.

Blaine shows up with another boy, who Jinx doesn't know very well. Oscar Ekland is tall and thin, with buzzed blond hair and a weird penchant for button-down oxford shirts, even in the humid summer heat. He moved from Sweden a little over a year ago when his dad got a job with the Swedish embassy in DC. He lives in one of the fancy modern town houses over in the Hyattsville Arts District, but he met Blaine at the Melrose skate park right after he got to the US, and kind of glommed on to him. That's pretty typical for Blaine. His chill, upbeat attitude seems to draw people to him.

"Sorry we're late, Jinxie." Blaine gives her a sunny smile that suggests it doesn't actually trouble him very much. "We were at Oscar's house and he had to do some chores before his parents would let him out."

Oscar makes a sour face. "Parents are such a pain."

Blaine glances worriedly at Jinx, but she's not going to make a fuss. This isn't the first time she's had to listen to other kids complain about their parents. She knows Oscar is just trying to sound cool and doesn't really mean anything by it. Of course, he *should* appreciate the fact that his parents are alive. That they can still hang out with him, and help him when he's in trouble, cheer him up when he's sad, or make sure he's getting enough to eat and taking regular showers. Not that *Jinx* needs help with that stuff anyway. She's fine. She has it all under control.

So she just ignores Oscar and instead asks Blaine, "So what do you want this shoot to be? Like, action shots?"

"Yeah, absolutely." He nods. "I had someone try to take some with their phone camera one time, but they all just came out blurry."

"Yeah, if the subject is moving fast, you have to increase the shutter speed," says Jinx. "But then you need a wider aperture, which could make the background super blurry, so *then* you need to bump up the ISO to compensate. But not too much, because the color saturation . . ."

She trails off when she notices Blaine giving her the raised eyebrow, which he does very well.

"You don't actually care," she says.

"Nope," he agrees cheerfully. "Just make it look cool. I trust you."

They begin the photo shoot. Blaine doesn't want Oscar in the shots, so the lanky Swede is goofing around in the shallow beginner bowl while Blaine drops in on the deeper, advanced bowl. He's only warming up, carving loose figure eights, but Jinx starts taking pictures anyway. She never knows what the perfect shot will be until she goes back and looks at the entire set, so it's best to take as many as possible. She has several extra SD memory cards if she fills up this one. Granted, she'll need at least some of those for her afternoon client, but she can go home in between and dump the images onto her computer to free up space.

After a few minutes, Blaine starts getting more serious. First with a couple of blunt to fakies, then some carve grinds and slash grinds on the edge of the bowl. His board scrapes loudly against the lip, followed by the rattle of his wheels as he comes back down. The sound abruptly cuts off when he does a frontside air, then resumes with a sharp smack of rubber on cement when he lands it.

By then, Jinx is in full photographer mode, not just taking the picture that's there but trying to anticipate the picture that's about to take place. It helps that she's been watching Blaine skate for as long as she can remember. She knows all his moves, his preferences, how he likes to do two tricks that he's very comfortable with, then follow up with one that he's still working on. He doesn't land them all and has to do a butt slide now and then. She captures it all in a frenetic series of snaps, taking hundreds of pictures in the space of a few minutes. She knows it will be a pain to go through them all later, but it's better to have too many shots than too few.

Truthfully, these "action" shoots aren't her favorite. She much prefers a static image, ideally indoors where she can control the lighting. The constant movement makes it difficult to predict the best framing, and the sun appearing and disappearing behind cloud banks changes the lighting constantly. There's so much to think about and adjust for every single moment, and she has to be "on" the whole time. It's really stressful. But she knows this is important to Blaine, and he is important to her, so she pushes through the frustration and anxiety until at last he decides to take a break.

They sit side by side on the rim of the bowl, sharing an energy drink that Oscar grabbed for them from the co-op. The thick summer heat has gotten stifling, and the metal can feels pleasantly cool in Jinx's hand. She stares down into the empty cement bowl, which is now streaked black with skid marks.

"Anything good?" Blaine asks.

She shrugs. "I'll send you the proofs and you can decide."

"Don't send me *everything* this time," he says.

"I know, I know."

"There were *thousands* last time."

"I'll narrow it down," she promises.

He thinks a moment. "Did you get any of the butt slides?"

"I got everything." To other people, that might sound like a boast, but Blaine knows she means it literally.

"Send me some of those, too," he tells her. "Like some funny embarrassing ones along with the cool ones."

She nods. "What are you going to do with these anyway?"

"Haven't decided yet," he admits. "But you owed me, so I wanted to collect."

This is how she agreed to pay him back for setting up her computer.

"Are we even now?" she asks.

"Hmm." He taps his lip thoughtfully. "Depends on how good these are."

She sighs. "I guess that's fair."

"Blaine, you ready?" Oscar calls from the other bowl. "We have to go soon."

"Yeah, we're good." Blaine stands up and stretches.

"Where are you going?" she asks.

"Teenager stuff. Don't worry about it."

"Technically, I'm *almost* a teen," she objects.

"Sure you are." He ruffles her hair playfully with one hand, then grabs his board. "See ya later, Jinxie."

She glares at his broad back as he walks away. She's annoyed that he ruffled her hair like she's some little kid. *Not* because he's leaving her out of whatever "teenager stuff" he has planned with Oscar, who's only known him for like less than a year. That's fine. It's whatever. She has more important things to do anyway.

3

THE PIZZA PLACE

Jinx packs up her camera equipment, making sure to carefully wipe the lens as always. Then she heads over to Joey's, a small pizza shop in Roosevelt Center by the co-op grocery store.

"Hey, Jinx," says Reese, the girl behind the counter. She's a senior in high school, so even older than Blaine. She has long, wavy brown hair and a gentle smile. She never treats Jinx like a kid, and Jinx will be sad when she goes off to college next year.

"Hey," says Jinx.

"The usual?"

"Yes, please."

Reese hands her a slice of cheese pizza on a paper plate. There are several tables with orange plastic tops, but Jinx eats while standing there at the counter. It's not that she thinks Joey's is dirty or anything. This is just easier and less stressful for her.

Behind Reese is a big menu board with images of pizza and calzones that Jinx took a few months ago. Instead of payment for that shoot, Jinx gets a free slice of pizza every time she comes in. This is what she means about having the food situation under control. She takes pictures for nearly all the local businesses, free of charge. And in return, she almost never has to pay for anything.

"Oh, Jinx, is that you?" Ms. Lombardi's voice comes from the back.

"Yep, it's me," calls Jinx.

Ms. Lombardi hurries out, her eyes wide with eagerness. She's a tall woman with long box braids pulled into a bun. She wears a white JOEY'S apron over her green T-shirt and tan shorts. Her husband's family, the Lombardis, have owned Joey's since before Jinx was born, and now Mr. and Ms. Lombardi jointly run the restaurant. At least supposedly. It seems to Jinx that Ms. Lombardi is there a *lot* more often than her husband.

"I want to add some new items to the menu," says Ms. Lombardi.

"So you want another photo shoot?" guesses Jinx.

Ms. Lombardi beams at her. "Such a smart girl. And honestly, it'll be good for you to eat something other than pizza every day."

Jinx disagrees, but keeps that to herself. "So what are we adding?"

"Subs!" Ms. Lombardi declares, then looks at Jinx expectantly.

"Uh . . . great?" Jinx ventures, although she can't see why anyone would order a sub when they can have pizza.

Ms. Lombardi heaves a dramatic sigh. "I know kids your age always want to eat the same thing all the time, but trust me, when you're a little older, you'll appreciate some variety."

Jinx shrugs. She's certainly not going to argue with one of her clients.

"I'd like to get images of maybe three different types of subs," says Ms. Lombardi. "A meatball sub to go with the Italian theme. Then maybe something a little healthier, like a veggie sub with hummus, olives, cucumber, tomatoes . . . Doesn't that sound delish?"

"Sure," Jinx says although it actually sounds like something she would never want to eat.

"And for the last one, I think a cheesesteak!" declares Ms. Lombardi.

"Is that even a sub?" asks Jinx.

Ms. Lombardi waves her hand. "Close enough. And I *am* from Philly, you know."

"Oh, cool," says Jinx, who hadn't known that. She'd like to visit places like Philly, someday. She has field trips, sure. Not just to DC. She's also been to Baltimore twice. But on field trips, the teachers are always telling her where to go and what to do. She can't just wander around taking pictures. She's asked Aunt Helen if they can go to, like, the Inner Harbor or something, but her aunt works so much that they never have time. Jinx doesn't get mad about that because she understands it's her fault that her aunt has to work so much. Kids are expensive, even if they can mostly feed themselves.

"So," says Ms. Lombardi, pulling Jinx out of her thoughts. "When can you fit me in?

"I'm booked up tomorrow, but how about Wednesday?"

"Perfect! Does ten a.m. work?"

"Okay." Jinx writes a reminder on her arm.

"You have a phone, right?" asks Ms. Lombardi.

"Sure."

"You should start putting appointments on the calendar app instead of just writing them on your arm."

"Thanks, but this works for me." Jinx could explain the system she has developed to remember and plan things, but she's noticed that people's eyes tend to glaze over after the first couple of minutes, so she mostly doesn't bother now.

"If you say so," Ms. Lombardi says dubiously. "How's your aunt, by the way?"

"She's okay. Things have been busy at the hospital, I guess."

Ms. Lombardi nods. "It's always something, isn't it?"

"Yep." Jinx has noticed adults like to say that a lot for some reason.

"Well, you give her my best, okay?"

"Will do," Jinx promises.

"Heading to another client now?"

"Yeah." Jinx makes a face. "Headshots."

4

THE ACTOR

Jinx has plenty of time before her next appointment, so she stops at the co-op to pick up a bottle of chocolate milk and some sunscreen, both of which are free because she does the photos for their weekly advertisements. Then she heads home to download the images from that morning onto her computer. RAW files are extremely large, and there are a lot of them. While she's waiting for them to transfer, she decides to take a shower. Summers in the DC area are always hot and humid, and she feels like she's constantly walking around with a layer of sweat coating her skin. It's not unusual for her to take two or even three showers a day during the summer. It's not a germ thing. She just feels better after.

But before she takes a shower, she copies the reminders from her arm to a whiteboard fixed to the wall by her desk. At the top is written:

Jinx's Week

Below that, it's divided into seven columns, one for each day of the week. There's something about being able to see the list of activities and appointments visually laid out for the week that she really likes. It makes everything feel a little more manageable.

By the time she's done with her shower, the images have all been imported to her computer. She doesn't look at any of them yet, though. She knows that once she starts, she won't want to stop, and right now she needs to focus on her next appointment. Headshots may be the most boring kind of shoots she does, but they're really important to the person getting them. Or . . . sometimes really important to the person's mother.

Jinx is pretty sure that's the case here. She's known Swapna Kapoor since kindergarten, and not once has she ever said she wanted to be an actor or model. But apparently, someone told Ms. Kapoor that her daughter could do really well in the industry. So for the last six months, Swapna has been auditioning for a bunch of casting calls in the DC area. She hasn't had any luck yet, but recently a casting director suggested that if Swapna really wants to get serious, she needs a professional headshot. When Ms. Kapoor found out how much a professional photographer would cost, she called up her daughter's classmate instead.

"Janessa, dear, you're as good as any professional!" she told Jinx over the phone last week, and Jinx could not disagree. So here she is, skating over to the Kapoor house for a photo shoot.

The neighborhood where Jinx lives is actually Old Greenbelt. It's a historic landmark area and still has all the original 1930s town house blocks and landscaping. Hardly anyone has a yard, and everything is nestled in among dense clusters of tall trees. But the Kapoors wanted one of those large freestanding homes with a grassy yard and a garage. So they live just outside the historic area in a more traditional suburban setting where people are allowed to have that kind of stuff. It's only four blocks from Jinx's house, but when she crosses the boundary, her surroundings look completely different. Everything is spread out, and there's no shade in sight. Jinx doesn't really get the appeal, but like a lot of things, she keeps that to herself.

She has to admit that the Kapoor house is very nice. It's about twice as big as Jinx's home, and yet it's always pretty clean. Except for the dog hair. Ms. Kapoor has two tiny, yappy dogs that she spoils outrageously, so it can't be helped. Jinx deals with it for short periods of time by reminding herself that she doesn't live there. She'll be able to return to her fur-free home soon enough. It's not like she gets invited over often anyway.

She arrives at the Kapoor house with her camera case, her tripod, and a large backpack that contains her "portable studio," which is essentially some clamp lights, a thin steel cable, and a gray drop cloth curtain.

Jinx knocks at the front door and Swapna opens it, the two little dogs barking around her feet. Swapna is taller than Jinx, and has long, glossy black hair that goes halfway down her back. Her heart-shaped face is very soft and warm-looking, and she's recently started wearing makeup. Jinx can understand why someone would say she could be an actor or model.

"Hey," says Swapna as she steps aside. "Sorry my mom is making you do this."

"She promised to feed me," admits Jinx.

The living room alone is roughly the size of Jinx's entire downstairs level. It has hardwood floors, which Jinx likes, but also thick, high-pile rugs that seem almost designed to trap dog hair. The furniture is mostly wood. Nice wood, too, not the pressed particle board IKEA stuff at Jinx's house.

Swapna's house also has central air conditioning, which none of the houses in Old Greenbelt have. Jinx is pretty sure there's a rule against it or something, which is a bummer. Window AC is fine, but she much prefers the cold crispness of central AC. Especially in the summer. She already wants to take another shower.

She gives Swapna an appraising look. "Are you nervous?"

Swapna shrugs but doesn't quite meet her eyes.

"It's just me, you know," Jinx tells her.

"I know . . ." says Swapna, although she doesn't look all that comforted.

"I remember when you used to stick crayons up your nose, so it's a little late to worry about impressing me."

Swapna gives her a sour look. "Hilarious."

"I'm only joking. You look way better than I ever could."

"Maybe if you made an *effort*, like wearing something other than those giant old T-shirts."

Jinx wants to say that they're her *dad's* shirts. That they're *special*. But that would mean talking about her dad, which she doesn't want to do. At all. With ⎰

Then Ms. Kapoor hurries into the room.

"Ah, Janessa, so good to see you!"

She swoops Jinx up in a big, motherly hug. Jinx bears it graciously. It's not that she *dislikes* hugs, but they're certainly not part of her daily routine.

"Good to see you, too, Ms. Kapoor."

"Look at all this equipment you have," Ms. Kapoor says excitedly as she gestures to the case and backpack. "Very professional looking!"

"I do my best." Jinx scans the living room for a suitable place to set up. But there isn't a lot here for her to fasten her cable to for the backdrop, and only a couple of windows. She peeks into the next room. "Can we set up in there?"

"The dining room?" asks Ms. Kapoor. "Whatever you think is best, dear."

Jinx's house doesn't have a dining room, but the Kapoor house has a big one with a bunch of windows to let in natural light. It also has several heavy pieces of wood furniture that are perfect to use as anchors for her backdrop. She attaches one end of the cable to a buffet, and the other to a long sideboard half covered in knickknacks that could use a good dusting. Then she throws the drop cloth over the cable, creating a simple backdrop for the shoot. After that, she drags an armless wooden dinner chair over and places it directly center, in front of the backdrop. Then she pats the seat and looks at Swapna.

"You're here."

Swapna nods and sits down in the chair while Jinx sets up her tripod and hangs her clamp lights. There isn't much artistry to it. Headshots need to be boring. No fancy lighting, no moody shadow, no forced perspective, no dynamic framing. Nothing at all that could distract from the subject. It makes perfect sense, given that the purpose of the image is to sell the person auditioning for a variety of roles. It needs to be neutral. But it's also what makes taking headshots extremely dull.

The only real challenge in taking headshots is the subject. Some people naturally know how to engage with the camera, and some people don't. Unfortunately, it takes Jinx all of two shots to decide that Swapna is one of the people who doesn't. She sits stiffly, almost flinching at every shutter snap. She looks self-conscious, guarded, and distrustful, not like someone a casting director would want to hire. Jinx needs to distract her, make her forget she's getting her picture taken. Then maybe she'll loosen up and be herself.

"What kind of acting do you want to do?"

"Huh?"

Snap

The question takes Swapna by surprise and she lets her guard down. But only for a moment. Jinx is going to have to keep distracting her, like a magician who misdirects your attention so you don't notice she's palming the coin.

"Like Shakespeare?" presses Jinx. "Or movies?"

"Oh, uh . . ." Swapna takes a moment to consider.

Snap

"I guess movies?"

"Action movies? Dramas? Horror?" continues Jinx. "I like horror best."

"That's because you're a weirdo."

The word stabs Jinx's chest like the big kitchen knife that Michael Meyers uses to kill people in the Halloween movies. She knows that she and Swapna aren't friends, of course. But she thought this was neutral turf and Swapna would talk to her like when they were in elementary school, not parrot the stuff that other kids in middle school say.

Jinx's hands squeeze her camera hard. She wants to say something nasty. She wants to say it must be *really great* to not be a weirdo. It must be *so nice* to have a big house with AC, and a mom who takes her on auditions and wherever else she wants to go . . .

But Jinx is a photographer and this is her subject, so she would never say something like that. As a photographer, it's important to see a good shot when it happens. And in this moment, what Swapna has just said makes her look confident. It's a good shot.

Snap

"Yeah, I'm a weirdo," Jinx says encouragingly, trying to bring out more of this self-assurance. Anything to get the good shots. That's what a photographer does. "I bet I'd make a good quirky sidekick in a horror movie."

"Don't they always die?"

Snap

"Usually."

Jinx keeps the stream-of-thought conversation going. It's pretty easy since she knows Swapna so well. It might have been harder with a different subject, but Jinx can get along with just about anyone when she makes the effort. A good photographer knows how to get the best out of her subject. No matter what.

5

THE RESET

After the photo shoot, Ms. Kapoor feeds them really good daal with rice, and even sends Jinx home with leftovers. The late summer sun is beginning to fall behind the tree line by the time she gets back to her house.

Her aunt has left a note on the fridge before heading to work:

J—

Make sure you eat something. Don't forget you have an appointment with Ms. Simmons tomorrow morning. We need to leave no later than 8:00 a.m.

Love, Auntie

The appointment isn't a surprise to Jinx. She has her trusty whiteboard, after all. But she heaves a sigh anyway because she never looks forward to these appointments.

She hangs up the backpack with her portable studio in the closet, then straightens up the house. It's not a mess or anything. But for some reason her aunt tends to move things around. A book here, a candlestick there. It's all just a little off. Her aunt doesn't push in her chair properly either. She also has a habit of leaving dirty dishes in the sink, which is just gross, so Jinx washes those as well.

When all that is done, Jinx takes a moment to savor her work. Everything is perfectly reset. Just as it should be. She knows her aunt will mess it up again when she comes home, but Jinx doesn't mind. Sure, she likes having everything in its proper place. But she also likes *putting* things in their proper places. Ms. Simmons calls it a coping mechanism, but whatever. It works, and it's not bothering anyone. Well, as long as she doesn't do it when her aunt is around. She learned pretty soon after she moved in that her aunt doesn't like to be reminded that she's a bit of a slob. Which is fair. So Jinx only does it when her aunt's not looking.

Now that the downstairs has been reset, Jinx heads upstairs. She starts the import process for the headshots, then takes one last shower for the day because she hates to get in bed knowing she still has the day's funk on her. After her shower, she puts on her old, threadbare My Little Pony pajamas (Rainbow Dash, of course). They're a little small on her, but nobody else ever sees it, so Jinx has decided the soft comfiness outweighs the embarrassment factor.

Once the photos have all imported, she begins combing through them to decide which to keep and which to delete. Normally she enjoys this task. She can see all the work she's done that day in a very real, concrete way. It's tedious, but it's also satisfying.

Well, normally it is. But not this time.

Because about a third of the way through the skate shoot, it appears.

The smudge.

The exact. Same. Smudge. Except this time, it's not just on one image. It's on a *bunch* of them. Right there, smack in the middle of the frame, as though there's something on the lens. Except she *knows* there wasn't because she *checked* before the shoot.

Jinx glares at it, her jaw clenched. This isn't right. It's . . . something just *doesn't make sense* here. She has to take a moment. What did Ms. Simmons say? When she starts to get upset, she just needs to breathe. So she closes her eyes and takes a slow, deep breath.

Okay. That feels a tiny bit better.

She looks at the image again and starts to feel upset again, so she quickly moves to the next image.

But that one has the smudge, too. And the one after that. She flips from image to image and sees it again and again, on both the pictures of Blaine *and* the pictures of

Swapna. Not all of them, thankfully. Maybe about half of the images in total. Yet even more confusingly, the smudged shots aren't consecutive. It appears for a few shots, then it's gone, then it comes back a few shots later. It doesn't make any sense at all, and Jinx is getting furious.

She needs to understand what's going on. Once she does, it'll be fine, because then she can fix it. So she starts comparing the smudged shots. She looks carefully at each one. Are they all the same color?

Yes. A murky black, like a splash of ink.

The same shape?

No, not exactly. Because from its first appearance in the skate park to its final appearance in the headshots . . .

The smudge is getting bigger.

6

THE AUNT

When Jinx comes downstairs the following morning, she sees her aunt Helen sprawled on the couch, watching some British period drama on TV. She's holding the plastic tray of a microwave meal with one hand, and waves her fork at Jinx with the other.

"Morning, kiddo!"

"Morning, Auntie," Jinx says sleepily. She shuffles into the kitchen and makes some cereal.

Her aunt pauses the pensive handsome Englishman on TV and gives Jinx a careful look.

"Did you get to bed at a reasonable time?"

"Of course."

This is technically true. Jinx *went* to bed at a reasonable time. She just didn't get to *sleep* until much later because she couldn't stop thinking about the smudge. Not only did it mess up a bunch of otherwise great pictures, there's something about it that unsettles her. The randomness of it? The fact that it's getting larger? She doesn't understand it. And if there's one thing she understands pretty well, it's photography. So what's going on?

"Hmm." Aunt Helen's eyes narrow, like she suspects Jinx is fudging the truth. "Well, I have the day off today, so I will make *certain* you get a good night's sleep tonight. And a decent home-cooked meal."

"Great."

Jinx sits at the table and begins eating her cereal. She doesn't mention that Ms. Kapoor's home-cooked meals are significantly better and probably healthier, too. These days she doesn't ever say anything that might upset her aunt. She can't be sure how well she'd handle it. Jinx

macaroni in a buttery sauce. Jinx likes all these things, but for some reason, seeing them first thing in the morning is kind of gross. She doesn't say that, of course.

"What did you do yesterday?" her aunt asks.

"I took pictures of Blaine at the skate park, then I did headshots for Swapna. Oh, and Ms. Lombardi says hi."

"How is she doing?"

Jinx shrugs as she eats a spoonful of cereal. "She's adding subs to the menu for some reason."

"I guess it'll be a change of pace."

"That's what she said. I'll stick with pizza."

"Enjoy it while you can," advises her aunt. "Your father and I both became lactose intolerant in our twenties, and now pizza isn't nearly as much fun. Pretty sure it's genetic, so that'll probably happen to you, too."

No more pizza? Jinx can't imagine a worse fate. Well, that's not true. She doesn't need to imagine a worse fate because she's already been through one. But pizza is one of the things that help a person deal with a terrible fate. To have something like that snatched away is like kicking them while they're down.

"What did Swapna need headshots for?" asks Aunt Helen.

"She wants to be an actor or something."

"Does she?" her aunt asks in surprise.

"Well, her *mom* does," amends Jinx. "I think Swapna is kind of on the fence about it. She's just going along with the whole thing."

Aunt Helen sighs. "Poor thing . . . Well, I guess it's not my place to judge someone else's parenting. We aren't exactly perfect."

"We're not?" asks Jinx.

Aunt Helen squints at her, like she isn't sure if Jinx is joking. Jinx isn't sure either. After a moment, her aunt shakes her head and smiles. Then she focuses on her dinner, which is fine by Jinx. Mornings are always a little tough because Jinx has sleepy waking-up energy and her aunt has frazzled end-of-the-day energy. They're in completely different modes.

After they finish eating, Aunt Helen rinses her plastic tray (although not thoroughly) and puts it in the recycling. Then she just tosses her fork in the sink, still half covered in food residue. Jinx washes her bowl and spoon, as well as her aunt's fork. Then, when her aunt goes upstairs to use the bathroom, Jinx fishes the tray out of the recycling and rinses it thoroughly before putting it back.

Jinx goes upstairs, but her aunt is still in the bathroom with the door closed. So she logs into her computer and posts one of the smudge-free pictures from yesterday to her @jinxphotography account online. It's a shot of Blaine doing a backside slash grind, his expression serene, totally in the zone. He looks extremely cool. Jinx has gotten a lot better at spotting which images in a set just *work*, and this is definitely one of them.

Once the bathroom door finally opens, Jinx approaches cautiously, armed with a bottle of air freshener. Aunt Helen is standing at the sink, brushing her teeth, and rolls her eyes at Jinx.

"It's not that bad," she says around her toothbrush.

Jinx sprays anyway. Because it is that bad. Then she brushes her teeth and applies some new Band-Aids to the fingertips that need protection, which at this point are most of them. These Band-Aids are light blue to match her T-shirt, which is another of her dad's vintage band shirts. The shirt is white, with the cover of Nirvana's *Nevermind* album on the front. It has a picture of a baby swimming in a pool as he reaches for a dollar bill on a hook. It's an amazing photograph, and her Band-Aids match the blue of the swimming pool perfectly.

"I really want you to make an effort with Ms. Simmons today," says Aunt Helen.

"I will."

She gives Jinx a hard look. "Will you?"

After a moment's thought, Jinx says, "I don't actually know what you mean. Like, I don't want to waste Ms. Simmons's time, or your money. But it's just . . . how do you actually *try* in therapy?"

Now it's Aunt Helen's turn to consider. "Hmm. I guess just talk to her. Be honest. Listen to what she's asking, and really think about it before you answer. Just like you and I are doing right now."

"Okay, I'll try that," she promises.

Aunt Helen smiles and briskly rubs Jinx on the back. "You're a good kid, you know that?"

Jinx shrugs. She's not so sure about that but isn't about to argue.

By the time they're both done with the bathroom, it's nearly eight, so they hustle downstairs and put on their shoes. Aunt Helen didn't used to leave her shoes at the door but decided to start doing it after Jinx patiently explained how much easier it would be to keep the house clean.

Once they're ready to go, Jinx grasps the doorknob, then tilts her body so that her aunt can't see her tap out the sequence.

Tappity-tappity. Tap. Tap. Tappity-tappity. Tap. Tap.

She's not ashamed that she does it. Not exactly. She just

doesn't want to talk about it, so it's better to keep it hidden. It's not like it's hurting anyone. It's just a weird little thing she does.

As Jinx opens the door, her aunt says, "Allons-y!," which means "Let's go!" in French. The only reason Jinx knows this is because when she was younger, she and her dad would come over to Aunt Helen's house and watch *Doctor Who* all the time, and that was something the Doctor always said. Now her aunt says it pretty much whenever they leave the house.

Is that really so different from what Jinx does? She's pretty sure it's not.

7
THE THERAPIST

Ms. Simmons's office is small and cozy. It's also stuffy and a bit cluttered. Not only on the desk but also in the shelves. Instead of just cramming every shelf with books, some of them are only half full of books while the other half hold little sculptures or candles. It could have been a visual mess, except Ms. Simmons has a good eye and everything comes together in a pleasing, balanced symmetry. And despite all the *stuff*, it's always impressively free of dust.

Ms. Simmons looks like she's in her late thirties, although she might be in her forties or even early fifties.

With some people, it's hard to tell. As far as Jinx is concerned, there isn't much difference anyway. Ms. Simmons has short hair and a long, elegant neck. She always wears bright colors, like lime, lavender, or tangerine, although, never all at once. Today it's a goldenrod pantsuit. She also has a bunch of jewelry. Rings, earrings, bracelets, and even a small nose ring. Jinx picked Ms. Simmons from the options on the health insurance website because of the nose ring, which is probably not a great way to select a therapist.

Thankfully, the nose ring promise was not a lie. Jinx *does* like Ms. Simmons. But that doesn't make it any easier to talk about stuff. They sit across from each other on comfy chairs. Ms. Simmons's slim hands are folded in her lap, and her posture is perfectly erect. Jinx is slouched into her seat about as far as she can go, Vans kicked out as far as *they'll* go. Her arms dangle off the sides as though she's fishing for finger-eating creatures who live in the rug.

"Janessa—"

"I prefer Jinx." Her aunt said be honest. She's being honest.

"Is that what your friends call you?"

"That's what *everyone* calls me." Be honest. "Well, some adults call me Janessa. But only the ones who didn't know my dad very well."

"Your father gave you that nickname?"

Jinx pauses as an unpleasant feeling flutters in her chest. This is the part where she would like to stop talking now, please. But she did promise she would try. "Yeah."

"Why do you think he gave you that name?"

She starts picking at one of her blue bandages. "Because it's a cool nickname?"

"It is a cool-sounding nickname," agrees Ms. Simmons. "Do you know what the word itself means?"

"Sure, it's like a hex. Dark magic. The Scarlet Witch and stuff."

"The official definition is a thing or person who brings bad luck."

A coldness drifts into Jinx's stomach. She doesn't like where this is going and begins pulling harder on her bandage. "Oh. Okay."

"Do you think your father knew that when he gave you the nickname?"

The coldness inside her deepens into ice. She can feel it crawling up her spine toward her throat, sharp and crackling. It's getting harder to talk. She has to make an effort to get out a few terse phrases.

"I don't know. Probably. He was really smart."

Ms. Simmons nods. Then she waits.

Jinx is pretty smart herself. She *knows* what Ms. Simmons is expecting her to say. That her father gave her that name because he thought *she* was bad luck. This is a hundred percent one of the things she doesn't want to talk about. Even thinking about it makes her words stick in her throat. So she sits without speaking as the icy cold from her gut fills her chest, her throat, her jaw, her teeth . . .

Ms. Simmons asks, "Are you a big music fan?"

"Huh?" The question catches Jinx off guard. Enough to make the jagged ice in her throat ease off a little.

Ms. Simmons points to the Nirvana T-shirt. "You always come in wearing a vintage band T-shirt. I think last time it was the Red Hot Chili Peppers. And the time before that . . . the Cure, I believe?"

"Oh, um, well, I like the photo for this one."

"That's right. You're a photographer."

"Yeah. It's my favorite thing to do." Jinx's throat loosens a little more. She's always ready to talk about photography. It's the most important thing for her. It's what makes her good.

"You started taking pictures because you wanted to learn how to use your father's camera, right?"

Her throat tightens again. "I guess so."

"And those are his T-shirts that you wear all the time, right? They're pretty big on you."

"It's the look." Well, it's *a* look anyway. Maybe not

currently the most trendy, but still. She's pretty sure that she makes it work.

"If I can make an observation," says Ms. Simmons, "you seem pretty uncomfortable talking about these things."

The icy strangle is back. Worse now. Like a frozen hand gripping her throat. Jinx says nothing.

"Janessa . . ." Ms. Simmons pauses and corrects herself. "Jinx, it's okay to admit that you miss your father."

Forget talking, now Jinx can't even breathe. Her brain is white static. Her hands grope for something. Anything. She tries to bite one of her nails, but nearly all are covered with pool-blue Band-Aids for precisely this reason. She wants to escape—this room, this building, this *feeling* inside her. It's too much. *It's all too much.*

Ms. Simmons leans across the narrow gulf between them and places her cool hand on Jinx's burning-hot cheek.

"You're okay," she assures Jinx. "You don't have to talk. You don't have to do *anything* except breathe. Do it with me, now. In . . ." She inhales. "And out . . ."

Jinx takes a slow, shaky breath.

"There now. That helps, right?" asks Ms. Simmons.

Jinx shrugs.

Ms. Simmons gives her a sad smile. "I promise you, Jinx. I will never make you talk about anything you don't want to talk about. Okay?"

Jinx swallows hard. "Okay."

It makes her feel a tiny bit better to know that. But it also makes her wonder. If she doesn't have to talk about the things she doesn't want to talk about it, then how does she actually "try" in therapy? And does she even want to, if it's going to feel like this every time?

8

THE COSPLAYERS

Aunt Helen looks pretty tired by the time they get home. Ten a.m. is way past her bedtime, after all. She offers to make Jinx some lunch, but Jinx says she already has plans. Aunt Helen nods sleepily (and maybe a little gratefully), then heads upstairs to bed.

Jinx wasn't lying. She *always* has a plan of some sort, and today the plan is to have lunch at Beijing Pearl Asian Bistro in Roosevelt Center. The restaurant is a large, open space with circular tables evenly placed throughout the room. Near the front door is the cash register and a small bar. Mr. Lo is polishing glasses behind the bar when Jinx comes up. He's a stocky man with only a circular crown of gray hair on his head.

"Good morning, Jinx," he says cheerfully. "What'll it be today?"

"Morning, Mr. Lo. The usual, please."

He gives her an annoyed look. "Pork fried rice *again*? We do have other items on the menu, you know."

"Why mess with perfection?" she replies.

He smiles ruefully, then heads back to the kitchen. Like Jinx, Mr. Lo is incapable of disagreeing with someone when they compliment him, and they know this about each other.

She takes her rice in a to-go carton and sits in Roosevelt Center Plaza, which is an open, cement courtyard enclosed by carefully pruned shrubs. Sometimes the courtyard hosts concerts or little craft fairs. But since it's midday on a regular Wednesday in the summer, there's only a couple of retired folks hanging out on the benches. The weather isn't quite as swampy as yesterday, and the sun feels a little gentler.

Jinx isn't great with chopsticks, but Mr. Lo always looks so pleased when she asks for them that she muddles through the awkward business of shoveling fried rice from the carton. The secret, at least for her, is to simply hold the container as close to her mouth as possible. Aunt Helen would probably call it bad manners, but her aunt isn't here, so Jinx isn't going to worry about it.

Once she's finished, she goes back into Beijing Pearl to wash up, then heads to the location where she's meeting her afternoon clients. Old Greenbelt is designed with a number of winding inner pathways between the trees and town house clusters. Jinx can easily walk anywhere in the neighborhood. There is one major street, Crescent Avenue, that separates most of the homes from Roosevelt Center. But the pathways follow cement tunnels that go *under* Crescent, so she doesn't even have to cross that street. This was great for Jinx when she was younger. She could walk down to the library and get books by herself without ever having to worry about traffic.

Now she's doing a shoot inside one of the tunnels. Even though she's early, her clients are already getting ready. Monica was born in Brazil but grew up in Greenbelt and used to babysit Jinx all the time when she was younger. Jinx has always thought she looks super glamorous, like a social media influencer or something. It was originally Monica's idea to hire Jinx for these shoots. The other three are people that Monica goes to grad school with. Tia has a dense short mohawk and a commanding voice. Bill is bald and *much* more soft-spoken. Seth has long, light-brown hair pulled back in a ponytail, and kind of a BO problem. But nobody seems willing to tell him about it. Or else they did and he doesn't care. It's an odd, mismatched group, but there is one thing that brings them together: dressing up in costumes inspired by the anime and game franchise *Battle Maidens*: *Extreme Metal Squad*.

This is the third shoot Jinx has done for them in the past year. They make their own costumes and go to conventions all over the country. Apparently they're pretty popular at these things. Whenever Jinx posts a picture online from one of their shoots, all four of them repost it, and for the next day or so, Jinx's phone buzzes constantly with notifications for likes and reposts. Maybe because they're so popular, they feel pressure to constantly come up with new costumes every time a Battle Maidens thing comes out. Last time, it was for the new season of the anime. This time it's apparently for the launch of a tie-in mobile game called *Extreme Maidens*.

"So the full title is *Battle Maidens*: *Extreme Metal Squad*: *Extreme Maidens*?" Jinx asks as she checks her light meter in a darker part of the tunnel. "Doesn't that seem a little . . . repetitive?"

"Great." Seth sighs as he buckles on a white plastic chestplate that has been painted to look like tarnished metal. "We're being judged by a twelve-year-old."

"Jinx is too young for *Battle Maidens*," Monica says defensively. She's wearing what looks like a metal bikini, with the addition of giant metal boots, big clunky gloves, and a tiara. Also a cape.

"Or we're too old for it," Tia says dryly. Somewhat confusingly, she's wearing a normal, boring business suit. Although she's also wearing a massive hi-tech helmet with swirling purple lights and a glowing visor. Maybe it would make sense if Jinx watched the show.

Bill doesn't actually wear the costumes. He's the one who designs and makes them. Instead, he quietly moves from one person to the next, checking a buckle here, a clip there, to make sure everything is set just the way it should be.

Once he's satisfied, he nods to Jinx. "Okay, we're ready."

"Do you have a shot list for me?" she asks.

Bill gives her a sassy smile. "Who do you think you're talking to, Ms. Jinx? Of *course* I do."

He hands her a printed list with a breakdown for each shot. Who's in it, what they're doing, and some ideas for framing it.

"How much do you want me to light the tunnel?" she asks.

"Only a little. We want the whole thing dark and gritty, like urban Gotham kind of thing. Especially for the Violet Reign shots."

"Violet Reign?" Jinx asks.

"Sorry, I mean Tia's character," says Bill. "I want those purple lights to be really punched up and ominous looking."

"Gotcha," says Jinx. "I can also tweak the saturation on those and see what you think."

"Man, Jinx," says Tia. "I love how you always go with the flow. You're like the coolest twelve-year-old I know."

She shrugs, feeling a little embarrassed. "I'm just a photographer."

"Not just *any* photographer," says Monica. "None

of us could make these look as good as you do."

Jinx glances down at her father's Canon 5D, feeling her face heat up. "It's a really good camera."

"Pretty sure it's not *just* the camera either," Seth says.

She really doesn't like being the focus of the conversation, and just shrugs.

"Okay, okay, can't y'all see you're killing the poor girl with kindness?" Bill waves them off. "Now let's get to work, Ms. Jinx!"

Jinx smiles gratefully. "You bet."

Discomfort aside, it's a fun shoot. At first, the three models are a little uptight, so Jinx has them explain their characters to her while she's continually snapping pictures. It's amazing to watch how, as they talk, they slowly start to take on the personality traits that they're describing. By the end, they seem much more comfortable, shouting out lines that the characters say, and generally having a good time with it.

Jinx finds it so interesting how some people can escape

themselves with these fictional characters. She would love to be able to do that. To be someone else. Someone fun and brave and free . . .

But she's not. She's just Jinx. And she always will be.

It's what she deserves.

9

THE PERSPECTIVE

When Jinx gets home, she quickly resets the house before her aunt wakes up. Then she takes a shower. It's too early for bed, of course, but she knows the layer of funk she got from the sweaty summer afternoon will distract her while she's editing the images.

Before she can get to work, though, Aunt Helen wakes up and seems determined to spend the evening with her. Her aunt even makes her specialty dinner: chicken breast stuffed with cream cheese and wrapped in bacon. Extremely greasy, but very delicious. Aunt Helen chews a few lactose pills before they eat.

Once they finish, Jinx washes the dishes and her aunt dries. Jinx never says this, of course, but they always do it this way because when Aunt Helen washes, she doesn't rinse thoroughly, and Jinx has no interest in tasting soap in her next meal.

"After this, let's watch a show together," says Aunt Helen as they work.

"What show?"

"How about the new season of *Doctor Who?*"

Jinx looks over at her, unable to formulate a response. They can't watch *Doctor Who*. Not with just the two of them.

It takes Aunt Helen a moment to realize that she's said the wrong thing.

"Uh, you know what, forget that idea."

Jinx wordlessly goes back to doing the dishes. She'll pretend it never happened.

Aunt Helen stands beside her, staring down at the dish towel in her hands.

"You know, kiddo," she says quietly. "We can't do this forever."

Jinx freezes, the water from the tap spilling over her hands as they grasp the plate she's been washing.

"Can't do *what?*"

It hangs there for a moment. Jinx regrets asking the question because she *does not* want to hear the answer. She doesn't want to know what her aunt thinks it is that they can't do forever, *like there's some kind of choice.*

But, thankfully, Aunt Helen just says, "Never mind."

They finish the dishes in silence. Then, while Jinx is carefully wiping down the counter (her aunt always makes a big mess while cooking), Aunt Helen asks, "Sooo is there anything *you* want to watch?"

Jinx considers a moment as she squeezes out the sponge and places it on the drying rack. "How about *Battle Maidens: Extreme Metal Squad?*"

Aunt Helen looks blankly at her. "Huh?"

"It's an anime."

"Oh, okay. I didn't know you were into that kind of stuff."

"I'm not really," admits Jinx. "But the clients I had today are really into it."

"Monica and her cool grad-student friends?" Aunt Helen asks shrewdly.

"Yeah. I thought I might as well check it out so I know what they're talking about."

"Sure, why not!" says Aunt Helen. "You know, waaay back in the day, your father and I would stay up late to watch . . ."

She glances at Jinx, and Jinx is staring at her because *Why does she keep bringing stuff like that up?*

Aunt Helen shakes her head and forces a smile. "Anyway, anime night it is!"

"Great," says Jinx.

The show is certainly interesting. And very theatrical. Lots of people loudly declaring things to one another, fists and teeth clenched, with lasers and explosions flying everywhere. Jinx is impressed by how closely Bill was able to reproduce the highly stylized costumes. She does not, however, get any closer to understanding what the show is actually about.

After watching an episode, she and her aunt turn to each other.

"Huh," says her aunt.

"Maybe we should have started with season one," says Jinx.

"You think it would have made a difference?"

"Probably not."

After *Battle Maidens*, Jinx goes up to her room to start working on photos. She spent so much time the previous night freaking out about the smudge that she didn't actually finish retouching the ones that came out smudge free. And now she has to work through a ton of *Battle Maidens* cosplay images, too. Since she has another shoot tomorrow at Joey's, she doesn't want to get too far behind. Having a backlog stresses her out.

Jinx is pretty terrible at social media, mostly because she doesn't care a whole lot. But Blaine convinced her to start using it to promote her photography, so she posts one image per day. Still, she doesn't comment on other people's stuff, or even really look at other posts, and she only checks in once or twice a day.

Now, before she begins work in earnest, she checks her app. She sees a bunch of likes and comments with heart emojis for the image she posted of Blaine. Even though he's the one who talked her into making an account, he hardly ever posts anything himself. Jinx has noticed that a bunch of teenagers follow her, and she's pretty sure they're all using her account to stalk Blaine.

That reminds her, she still needs to send him his images. She looks over at her Daily board to see what else needs to happen. In addition to her "Jinx's Week," she also has a separate whiteboard labeled "Jinx's Day" that only shows what needs to happen today. Because even something as simple as "send pix to Blaine" is actually a multistep process that involves editing the images, selecting the best ones, uploading them, then sending the email. Four steps to complete one task. She doesn't have room to break things down into that much detail on her Week board, so each morning she copies that day's column from her Week board to her Day board, and expands each task to list all the actions she needs to take. It's a pretty obvious thing to do, when you think about it.

She pulls up her image folder, which of course is carefully organized into subfolders with the date and project title. Selecting which images to send to Blaine isn't actually that challenging because so many of them are ruined by the smudge. The same is true for Swapna's headshots. It's annoying, but since she took a bunch for both projects, there are plenty left to choose from. None of Blaine's butt slides survived the smudge, but he only asked for those as an afterthought, so he probably doesn't care all that much about them anyway.

Once she's finished sending links to Blaine and Swapna,

she turns her attention to today's images. It was a long shot list, so she knows it's going to take a while to get through them all. That's fine, though, because she's really in the zone. She's ready to get in there and tweak hundreds, or even thousands, of photos. After the stress she had this morning, it's going to feel great.

But then she opens the first cosplay image.

"No . . ."

Jinx launches out of her chair, but it's a tiny room so there isn't really anywhere to go. She paces back and forth a few times.

"No, no, no . . ."

She wants to bite her nails but they're all covered. She tries to scratch at her scalp, but the bandages prevent that, too. It's the other reason she wears them. She shakes her hands in helpless frustration and creases her face into a grimace. She wants to . . . She wants to . . .

It *doesn't matter* what she wants to do. Because she needs to calm down. *Seriously.* So she takes a slow breath, then forces herself to sit back down and look at the smudge. Which has gotten even bigger.

She clicks through image after image. It's not just on some of them this time. It's on *most* of them. Too many to cherry-pick from the ones that don't have it. Whole segments of the shoot are smudged. She's going to need to edit out the smudge, which is a slow and tedious process. Normally, she doesn't mind retouching, because she feels like she's making a good thing better. But this time she feels frustrated, almost *resentful*. She didn't put the smudge there, yet she has to spend all evening cleaning it up.

What if her camera is glitching? Or what if there's a dead spot on the mirror? Something like that would be expensive to fix, and she has no money. She can't ask Aunt Helen for something like that. Her aunt is already working so hard, such long hours. So what should Jinx do? How can she be a good photographer without a good camera? It's impossible.

But wait—if there's something wrong with the mirror,

why would it only show up sporadically? That doesn't make any sense. So that's probably not it. Then what? Every time she looks at the smudge it upsets her in a way she can't really articulate. Is she feeling anger? Fear? Both at once? She doesn't know. All she knows is that something about both the smudge and the feeling is just . . . *wrong*.

Yet there *has* to be some explanation, right? So even though she hates looking at the smudge—even though it makes her stomach squirm in a really uncomfortable way—she goes back and looks at it, image by image.

She notices that, just as in the previous batches, the smudge continues to get a tiny bit larger with each shot. It's not becoming clearer, which is weird, but the outline *is* shifting. In fact . . .

The smudge is zoomed in so far that it takes up the entire computer screen. Jinx zooms it out to get a little perspective. She goes back to the first image with the smudge, switches to slideshow view, then starts it up. The images change every few seconds, ice cream, skateboarding, headshot, cosplay . . . The smudge holds in the center for several shots in a row, then flickers out for one or two, then reappears. The edges are hazy at first, but picture by picture, they coalesce, growing sharper and more certain. Until finally the smudge becomes a clear, recognizable shape.

It's a person.

Jinx's skin prickles as she stares at the figure. It floats in the middle of the image, completely disconnected from everything around it, like some kind of dark specter.

Then she thinks, *Wait, if it's a person instead of a random smudge, maybe it's not getting bigger.*

Maybe it's coming closer.

10

THE SUBS

Jinx stands next to one of the orange Formica tables in Joey's. She wears a black T-shirt that says DEATH TO THE PIXIES in large white letters. It has a photo of the lead singer of the Pixies, Black Francis, lying on the ground while giving a thumbs-down gesture. Is it meant to be ironic? Self-loathing? Both? The Pixies aren't telling. Today Jinx's Band-Aids are olive green. They don't necessarily coordinate with the shirt; she just realized that she has a lot of green Band-Aids to use up.

She's already set the clamp lights around the table to provide a nice, bright atmosphere with almost no shadow.

Normally, she would still be fussing over them, tweaking the angles until it's absolutely perfect. But instead, she stares down at the camera in her hands as though it's haunted.

Is it?

"Okay, Jinx, you ready for the first item?"

Ms. Lombardi's voice snaps Jinx out of her reverie. She sees the pizza shop owner and Reese come out from the kitchen with trays of meatball sub sandwiches.

"I wasn't sure of the best way to present them," says Ms. Lombardi. "So we made a few variations."

The differences are minor. A little more sauce on one, a little less on another. There are some varieties in the bread choice as well. None of it looks great. Probably because it's edible. That's the thing about food photography. To get food that looks like a professional advertisement, it needs to be something you would never actually eat. The meat is never actually cooked, just browned on the outside. That's why it looks so juicy. Buns are often brushed with a plastic coating to give them a pleasing texture. Even the drops of "moisture" that supposedly run down the side of a nice refreshing beverage are little dollops of glue stuck to the side of the glass. There are a million tricks to make food look presentable enough for commercial photography, and a lot of them also make the food inedible.

While Jinx has heard about many of the techniques that food stylists use, she doesn't know how to do most of them, and doesn't have the materials she would need. So she carefully examines her options, and picks the one she thinks will work best. Or maybe the least-bad option, as her aunt would say.

Once she selects the sub and arranges it on the table, she makes a few adjustments to the lights, then mounts her camera on the tripod. She's about to snap the first set of images, but then pauses, her finger hovering over the button.

What if the smudge shows up again? What if it still looks like a person? What if it's even closer this time? If it moves every time she takes a picture, does that mean she'd have to stop taking pictures? *Could* she stop taking pictures? What does it even mean that the smudge person is getting closer? Could it get so close that—

"Jinx? Everything okay?"

Once again, Ms. Lombardi's voice pulls her out of an inner panic spiral. Jinx can't let her down. She can't let Joey's down. This place is an *institution*. That's how her father always described it. An essential part of Greenbelt.

"Yeah, I'm fine," she lies. "Just don't want to rush. I know how important this is for you."

"Don't stress it, Jinx," Reese says reassuringly. "You always do such a great job."

Jinx really is going to miss her when she goes to college.

"Okay, here we go."

She takes a deep breath and snaps the first image.

Normally, she leaves the display turned off on the back of the camera. It's not a good way to line up a shot, and it's distracting. But now she turns it on. Just to check.

No smudge.

She sighs in relief.

"Looking good?" Ms. Lombardi asks.

"Looking great," Jinx tells her truthfully.

Not perfect, but at least free of possibly supernatural shapes.

Feeling a lot better, Jinx dives into the shoot with her usual focus and quiet enthusiasm. They try a couple of different angles, and even swap in one of the other sample subs just to have some options. Every once in a while, Jinx pauses to check the display on the back of the camera. Each time, it remains smudge free.

Really, what was she thinking? A haunted camera? The idea is silly. *Childish* even. She knows better than to jump to conclusions like that. Her dad always said she had a good head on her shoulders.

Once Jinx has taken a bunch of shots, Ms. Lombardi and Reese hurry back into the kitchen to prepare the veggie sub. While she's waiting, Jinx sits at the table and picks at the abandoned meatball subs with a fork. They're pretty cold by now, but she doesn't mind that so much as she does the sauce, which is messy. She uses the fork to pluck out a meatball from the sodden, red-stained bun.

During her careful meatball extraction, Blaine strolls into the restaurant.

"Oh, hey, Jinxie," he says. "Doing a shoot for Joey's?"

She nods. "They're adding subs for some reason."

"Subs are better travel food," he says. "You can't wrap up a slice and shove it in your bag for later."

"That's a good point," she concedes. "Did you look at your photo set?"

"Yeah, they're great." He comes over and picks up a sub, heedless of the drippy mess. "These up for grabs?"

"Yup."

He takes a big bite, spreading sauce all over his mouth. Jinx's hands twitch as she fights off the urge to grab a napkin and wipe his face. She's been told in no uncertain terms that doing so is not okay and one hundred percent a violation of his personal space.

"By the way—" he says around a mouthful of meatball sub.

"Ugh, wait until you finish chewing." She makes a face and looks away. It's just too gross. And if there is one person in the universe she doesn't worry about offending, it's Blaine.

After taking a moment to chew and swallow, he says, "*Anyway*, I thought you were going to send me some butt slide shots."

"Oh, uh, they were all messed up."

"It's okay if they don't look great," he says. "I just want them for a laugh."

"No, they're . . ." She struggles with how to explain it to him without sounding like either a ridiculous fussbudget or a paranoid kook. "I think there was like a glitch in my camera. A bunch of shots got messed up."

His eyes widen. "Your *dad's* camera?"

She nods.

"Then we have to take it somewhere to get fixed," he says firmly.

"I think it's okay now," she says. "Whatever was going on, it's not happening anymore."

"You sure?" he asks.

"Yeah. It's good now. I double-checked before we started this shoot."

"Okay, cool," he says. "I know how important that camera is to you. If anything gets funky with it, let me know and we'll sort it out."

She smiles, feeling a little embarrassed by his protective, brotherly tone. "Thanks."

Ms. Lombardi and Reese come out with a platter of veggie subs.

"Oh, hey, Blaine," says Ms. Lombardi. "Scavenging the photo shoot?"

He grins impudently at her. "You know me so well, Ms. Lombardi."

She nods to the tray of cold meatball subs. "Well, have it all if you want."

"Sweet." He picks up the tray and slides into a nearby table. Eating two and a half meatball subs is no problem for him.

Ms. Lombardi lays the tray of veggie subs on the table. "Okay, I've tried some different arrangements with this one."

Jinx looks them over carefully. This is the moment she wishes she had some of those glue dewdrops. Fresh vegetables always look better with some water droplets. Or what *appear* to be water droplets anyway. She'll just have to do the best she can, as usual.

She refocuses her camera, then, as an afterthought, turns on the back display to check the last shot she took.

There's the meatball sandwich.

And right in the center is the smudge.

Jinx stares at it, feeling the tickle of panic rising at the back of her throat. She takes a calming breath. Okay. It's okay. The glitch or smudge or whatever is still there.

Surprising, but she hadn't checked this last picture, so she hadn't noticed. And it's frustrating, for sure. But, hopefully, most of the shots are okay.

Just to make sure, she scrolls backward on the display.

And it's there.

The smudge.

On every. Single. Shot. *Even that first one.*

Nothing makes sense anymore. Her face feels strangely cold, and the room airless. She tries another calming breath, but this time it isn't coming. Her lungs are locked. Her chest is heaving but nothing is getting through.

"Jinx?" Ms. Lombardi gives her a worried look. "You feeling okay?"

"You look really pale," agrees Reese. "Maybe you should sit down."

But Jinx can't sit because Jinx can't breath. There's no oxygen in this place. It's a vacuum. If she even opens her mouth, it will turn her inside out. She has to escape. She has to get air. She has to *get away.*

"Sorry, I . . ."

She detaches her camera from the tripod with numb, clumsy fingers.

"I can't . . ."

Then she runs out of the pizza shop.

11

THE OTHER TUNNEL

There is a path from Roosevelt Center, beyond the tennis courts and the baseball diamonds. It leads through a wooded area alongside an aqueduct, then into a small clearing with a firefly sanctuary and the occasional deer or fox. Beyond that clearing is a tunnel that cuts beneath Hillside Road. Not a wide cement tunnel, like the one from the cosplay shoot. This tunnel is narrow and made of corrugated metal. It's always dark and cool in there, even in the middle of a hot summer day.

This is where Jinx goes to feel normal again. Or as

normal as she ever feels. She sits on the cold cement ground with her back to the curved metal side, vehemently ignoring the fact that she's getting grime on her bottom. She pulls her knees in to her chest, wraps her arms around her shins, and interlaces her fingers. Then she squeezes as hard as she can until her shoulders ache. Until her fingers tingle with numbness. Until she feels like she can finally breathe again.

Blaine shows up soon after. He knew she'd be here. He also knew she'd need some time to herself before he arrived, so he didn't hurry.

He plops down beside her, and they sit in the cool darkness for a few moments.

"So what's up?" he asks.

"It's back," she mutters into her kneecaps, feeling denim threads tickle her lips.

"The glitch?"

"I don't know if it's a glitch," she says. "It looks like . . ."

She hesitates.

He waits.

She doesn't know how to say it.

Finally, Blaine asks, "How long have we known each other?"

"My whole life?"

"And have I ever said anything dumb to you?"

"Many times."

"Exactly. So whatever you're afraid to say, it can't be worse than some of the stuff I've said."

"What if it is?"

"Then obviously you'll have to stop complaining when *I* say dumb stuff," he says in a reasonable tone. "That's just fair."

She wants to tell him. He's normally the one person (still alive) that she never holds back from. So what's stopping her?

Fear. That this might change their friendship. Ruin it. That she might lose him, just like she loses everyone.

"Please tell me?" he asks.

He never says please. It's too much.

She sighs. "The glitch or whatever. It looks like a person."

"Huh?"

"See for yourself."

She picks up her camera from where it's been nestled in her lap, turns on the display, and gives it to him. She doesn't normally just hand her camera over to people, but this is Blaine.

The display faintly lights up his face in the dark tunnel as he looks through the pictures. His eyes slowly widen.

"That is just . . . *creepy*."

This simple statement sends a flood of relief through Jinx. It feels like every muscle in her body unkinks all at once.

"*Right*?" she says, exasperated.

"And you have no idea what's causing it?" he asks.

"None."

He nods, frowning thoughtfully. "Well, obviously we have to take it to someone."

"Like an exorcist?" she asks.

"No, Jinxie, like a camera shop."

12

THE CAMERA SHOP

They walk back to Blaine's place first. The town house clusters in Old Greenbelt are typically two sets of six that face one another, with a small parking lot between them. Each of these clusters is called a court, and each court has its own kind of vibe. Like a mini neighborhood within the larger neighborhood. Blaine's court used to also be Jinx's court, before she moved in with her aunt.

Some of the town houses in Greenbelt are brick, some are cinder block, and some are wood frame houses covered in vinyl siding. Each court sticks to the same type of structure but varies in color from one home to the next. The

Chen house is light blue vinyl with a white front door. Out front is a small garden that Ms. Chen has been obsessing over as long as Jinx can remember. In fact, Ms. Chen is out there working on it when they arrive. She's a slender woman with a short black bob. She's currently dressed in her gardening uniform of coveralls, straw hat, canvas gloves, and bright blue Crocs.

As they draw near, she looks up and says, "Xinyu, fetch me the shears, please." She has a British accent because she's from Hong Kong and learned English while studying in the UK.

"Sure," says Blaine. Xinyu is his Chinese name. It's pronounced "Zheen-shu," something that took Jinx a long time to get right.

"Wait here," he tells Jinx, and ambles into the house.

Ms. Chen watches him go, then mutters wearily, "No, please *do* take your time, my son. No need to hurry on your mother's account." Then she smiles at Jinx. "Hello, Janessa, dear."

It's not that Ms. Chen doesn't know she prefers to be called Jinx. She just thinks it sounds like "something you'd name a cat," and refuses to use it.

"Hey, Ms. Chen."

"How's your aunt?"

"She's okay. Working a lot."

"Not too much, I hope? She does have *other* responsibilities now."

"She cooked me a great dinner last night," Jinx says quickly.

Ms. Chen regards her carefully for a moment, then nods. Sometimes, Jinx gets the impression that Ms. Chen doesn't totally believe that Aunt Helen can handle parenting. Sometimes Jinx wonders if she's right.

Blaine comes back out with the hedge clippers and hands them to his mother.

"Can I borrow the car?"

"Why?"

"Jinx's camera is glitching, so I want to take her to a shop and have them look at it."

"The camera?" Ms. Chen frowns in concern. She also knows how important it is to Jinx. "How far away is the place?"

"I just looked it up," says Blaine. "It's over in College Park. By the Rita's."

"I guess that's okay. Just don't go anywhere else."

"Except Rita's?" He gives her a hopeful look.

She rolls her eyes. "I *suppose* Rita's is okay since it's right there. But you had better bring me back a chocolate salted caramel."

"Are you paying for it?" he asks.

Ms. Chen gives him a hard look. "Are you paying for the *gas?*"

He winces. "Never mind. Ice cream's on me."

"I thought so."

Blaine and Jinx head to College Park, which is the next town over from Greenbelt but only a fifteen-minute drive away. All the little towns are just satellites of DC, really. A large portion of College Park is taken up by the University of Maryland, but there's also a bunch of restaurants and stores off campus.

They pull into a somewhat seedy-looking parking lot with a line of stores, including a small pet hospital and a check-cashing place. The sign for the camera shop just says GEORGE'S CAMERAS in simple block letters.

It's pretty small inside, with a long wooden counter in the back. There are a bunch of cameras on display behind a glass cabinet off to one side. On the other side is a bookcase filled with stuff about photography.

A middle-aged man sits behind the counter, looking at a computer monitor. He has long dreads pulled into a ponytail, and he's wearing a brightly colored Tour de France T-shirt.

When they enter, he looks up from his computer. "Hey, kids, what can I do for you?"

"My friend's camera is kind of glitching," says

Blaine. "We were hoping you could take a look at it."

"Glitching?" the man asks.

Blaine nods to Jinx. "Show him."

She reluctantly holds out her camera to the man. She's not comfortable giving it to a stranger, but she recognizes that he may be her best shot at fixing it.

The man accepts the camera with an appropriate level of care. "I'm George, by the way."

"Jinx," she says shyly.

He nods appreciatively down at the camera. "Canon 5D Mark III. Very nice."

Jinx decides maybe he's okay. "My dad gave it to me."

"It makes me happy to see young people using a proper camera. Most of them just use their phones these days."

"Phone cameras are nice," admits Jinx. "But they don't have enough manual control. And they have that weird fake depth-of-field thing. Plus, you can't change the lens."

George smiles broadly at her. "I like you already, Jinx. Now, what am I looking for?"

"Turn on the display," she says. "You can scroll through. They're all like that."

He lights up the display and frowns at what he sees. He looks at a few more, and his unease grows. Then his eyes suddenly widen and he bursts out in a laugh.

"Man, you two had me going there for a minute. How'd you do it? Slow shutter speed with some overexposure, or what?"

Jinx and Blaine look at each other in confusion.

George catches this. "Oh, wait, this was an accident?"

Jinx feels her face heating up. She picks at her olive-green Band-Aids and looks down at her shoes. She's not used to feeling like such an amateur.

Blaine steps in, looking a little protective. "Yeah, it was an accident."

George holds up his hands in a placating gesture. "Sorry, my bad. I thought you two were trolling me. Because these are like those old spirit photographs, you know?"

Jinx doesn't know. "Spirit photographs?"

He nods eagerly. "Sure. You haven't heard of them?"

She shakes her head.

"Oh, cool. Let me show you."

He looks even more excited as he comes from behind the counter and goes over to the bookcase. He scans the shelves for a moment, then pulls out a large coffee-table book and starts paging through it.

"So, back in the mid-1800s, people started really getting into the idea of trying to communicate with the dead. Seances, spirit mediums, stuff like that. They called it Spiritualism, and it was like a huge craze, right? And at that same time, photography was still pretty new. Not a lot of people did it, or understood how it works."

He opens the book wide to a specific page and lays it flat on the counter for them to look at. It shows a sepia-toned photograph of a woman dressed in very old-fashioned clothing. She's just sitting and looking off to the side. A little girl stands beside her, but the girl looks weirdly faded. Translucent, like a ghost.

"So there was this dude . . ." George checks the caption for the photo. "William Mumler, that was it. He starts saying he has this psychic ability to take pictures of people that can show their dead loved ones hanging out with them."

"And people believed him?" asks Blaine.

"Sure. Photography was so new back then, people thought maybe *anything* was possible. So they paid good money to get their picture taken by this dude in hopes that their deceased uncle or mother or whoever would be chilling in the background. Maybe then they could feel just a little bit like they'd been reunited with that person."

Jinx scowls. "So he was taking advantage of them? Didn't he get in trouble?"

"Sort of," George says. "They put him on trial, but a bunch of real respectable people came to his defense. Arthur Conan Doyle even wrote a whole thing defending him."

"The *Sherlock Holmes* guy?" asks Blaine.

George nods. "Weird, right? His most famous character never believed in supernatural stuff, but he did. Anyway, they couldn't figure out how Mumler faked the images, so he was acquitted."

"How *did* he do it?" asks Jinx.

"We can't say for sure, but probably by reusing a plate. In those days, images were captured on a thin glass plate covered in silver bromide, which you then developed into the actual photograph. So he probably took one image ahead of time, then used the same plate when the customer came to get their photo taken, which would overlay the new image onto the old one. And because the first image was so faded and ghostly, the person couldn't really say for sure whether it was the person they actually knew. As long as it looked close, that was good enough for them."

"But how did he make the original person look like a ghost?" asks Jinx.

"Back then, there was only one shutter speed," says George. "Very, *very* slow. A person had to sit for a long time, perfectly still, to get the image to turn out right."

"So it just didn't have a long-enough exposure?"

"Probably," agrees George. "And sometimes he would even make images where the ghost seems to swirl past, which was likely the person slowly walking past the camera during the exposure time. See, that's one of the amazing things about photography. People think it's just a single moment frozen in time. But whether it's several milliseconds or several minutes, it's actually a *span* of time, all compressed and flattened into a single image."

"Like it's . . . *outside* of time?" asks Jinx.

"When you think about it like that," says George, "it's no wonder some people believed it could show a dimension of reality beyond our own."

Jinx's mind is a welter of new knowledge and feelings. Photography as a portal to the afterlife? As a portal to her *father*? What is it she's feeling? Hope? Fear? It's all so much. She has a difficult time managing it all. Coming here was supposed to make her feel better, but it's making her feel worse. She wants it to stop. She wants to snatch her camera from George and run out of the store, but that would be rude. He wouldn't like that. Maybe he wouldn't like *her*. This is a real, professional photographer and she *wants* him to like her. So she forces herself not to grab the camera, not to run. Instead, she just stands there, jaw clenched, knees locked, arms hugging herself as hard as she can.

Blaine catches her shifting mood and puts a reassuring hand on her shoulder. Then he looks almost pleadingly at George. "So what's wrong with her camera?"

George shakes his head sheepishly. "Oops, sorry, right. I got a little carried away there. Honestly? I'm not sure. I've heard of weird digital camera glitches. But they're rare, one-off things, not something that happens to every single photo in a shoot like this. Not on accident."

He pauses a moment to take in Jinx, who is almost quivering with suppressed anxiety, and Blaine, who looks desperate to sooth her. Then he sighs.

"Tell you what. Let me take a look at it tonight. Run

some diagnostics. If I can't find anything, I won't charge you."

"So you need to keep it?" Jinx wrestles with both the hope that this could be a solution, and the sacrifice it will require with no guarantee of success. "For how long?"

"Depends on whether I find something to fix, and what it would take to fix it."

Jinx gnaws on her bandaged finger.

"It's not like you can use it in this state anyway, right?" says Blaine. "Might as well see if he can do something."

She nods. "Yeah, I guess."

"Thank you," Blaine tells George. "This camera is really important."

"I'll do what I can," promises George.

13

THE TRUTH

Once they leave George's shop, they drive over to Rita's Italian Ice, which is not nearly as close as Blaine made it out to be when he told his mom. Rita's is open for only half the year, and they only have outdoor seating, at picnic tables. There's almost always a line, and today is no different.

Jinx gets a cherry Italian ice because for some reason Italian ice makes her feel slightly less like she's betraying Mr. Alsobrook's I Scream 4 Ice Cream truck, which comes to Greenbelt every Sunday for the farmers' market. Blaine gets an orange frozen custard, because he is a strange human.

All the tables are full, so they end up sitting on the curb. Jinx is pretty sure the seats at the picnic tables are just as dirty, so it doesn't bother her too much.

"Remind me to grab my mom's chocolate salted caramel on the way out," says Blaine.

Jinx nods.

"So . . . you think George can fix your camera?" he asks.

Jinx doesn't answer. During the drive from the camera shop, an idea slowly began to take hold in her mind. She doesn't think it's a good idea, but it keeps coming back to her anyway, again and again. It's like when she sees something in the house out of place but has to wait until her aunt leaves the room before she can fix it. A nagging irritation that slowly grows more insistent until it becomes almost painful.

"Jinxie?" prompts Blaine.

She doesn't want to give the thought shape, but she knows that if she does, she'll at least feel some relief.

So she asks, "What if it doesn't need to be fixed?"

"How do you mean?"

"I know all that spirit photography stuff was fake. I *know* that." She focuses on her cherry red Italian ice so she doesn't have to look at him. "But I can't help wondering if . . . you know . . ."

She can't finish. So close, but it's too much. Thankfully, she doesn't need to.

"If it's *him?*" asks Blaine.

"It was his camera after all. So maybe . . ."

She takes a bite of Italian ice so she won't have to continue. She knows the idea that her father might try to come back to her through the camera is ridiculous, childish, fairy-story kind of stuff. She wishes she could rid herself of it. But she can't.

They eat their Italian ice and frozen custard in silence. Jinx listens to the other people chat as they eat their own frozen treats. Their voices have a lightness and ease that Jinx doesn't feel. Maybe has never felt.

"Have you . . ." Blaine pauses, like he's trying to figure out the best way to say something. "Have you ever told anybody what you saw? That day?"

Jinx slowly pushes her spoon through the remaining red slush in her paper cup.

"They all *know* what I saw." The anger in her tone surprises her. "They just want to hear me *say* it."

"Maybe they think it'll make you feel better?" suggests Blaine.

She gives him a bitter look. "Maybe it'll make *them* feel better."

Blaine doesn't respond. Instead, he goes back to his frozen custard, which is a relief. Jinx knows she can count on him not to press her too hard on the thing that everyone else seems completely obsessed with. Like, if she just talks about it, that'll somehow make it all better. It won't make anything better. And even worse, she'll have a *new* memory of seeing their reactions. She'll have to witness it all over again through someone else's eyes.

"Okay," Blaine says finally. "I honestly don't know if I believe in ghosts or whatever. But just for a moment, let's say it *is* him. What do you think he wants?"

"Wants?" Her hand grips her spoon hard.

"That's the deal with ghosts or spirits, right?" points out Blaine. "They've been wronged somehow in life, so they come back to haunt people until that wrong is made right."

"I . . . guess." She stabs the red slush with her spoon.

"So who wronged your dad?"

She stabs it again. And again. And again . . .

"Jinx?"

Jinx: a person or thing that brings bad luck.

"You okay?"

A person who brings bad luck.

"Whoa, seriously, Jinxie, what's going on?"

Jinx continues to stab the dripping red slush as she whispers, "I know who wronged my dad."

"Forget about that," Blaine says hastily. "I shouldn't have brought it up."

She suddenly stops stabbing and looks at him. Her eyes are wide, and her next words come out like a strangled hiss through clenched teeth.

"It's me. *I* wronged him."

14

THE THEATER

This is Jinx's first day without her camera since her father's death. She doesn't like it. She doesn't know what to *do*. She feels anxious, like something bad is going to happen but she can't predict what.

She goes to Joey's and apologizes to Ms. Lombardi for running out in the middle of the shoot. The pizza shop owner seems more concerned than mad. Jinx almost wishes she *was* mad, because the worried look in her eyes makes Jinx even more uncomfortable. People often give her that look, usually when they think she won't notice. She *always* notices, but usually, she can ignore it by focusing on camera stuff. Now her hands are distressingly empty.

After she leaves Joey's, she decides to see a movie. Maybe it will distract her from how much she misses having her camera. The local theater looks just like it did in the 1930s on the outside, including the original sign, which spells GREENBELT down the front in vertical neon letters.

Since it's the middle of a weekday, there's no one at the box office window. Jinx walks into the lobby, where she's greeted by the smell of fresh popcorn, and Ms. Linkenholker behind the concession counter.

"Hey, Jinx. It's been awhile," she says. "How are you?"

"Oh, uh, okay I guess." That's not true, of course, but she's trying to distract herself from her problems, not talk about them even more. "Is there a movie soon?"

"Yep. *North by Northwest* starts in about thirty minutes."

"Cool, I guess I'll see that."

"It's kind of an old movie, but Hitchcock was one of the greats. I think it holds up pretty well."

Jinx nods. She thinks she's heard that name before, although she can't really remember from where.

"You want some popcorn?" asks Ms. Linkenholker.

"Sure."

Ms. Linkenholker fills a small bag and hands it to her. "Enjoy!"

"Thanks," Jinx says, then walks through the lobby and into the auditorium. While the outside looks old-fashioned, the inside is more modern, with comfy red seats and a giant screen. But there's still some vintage touches, too, like the curtains along the sides.

There aren't many people, which makes it easy to spot Swapna sitting in row G near the center. Jinx decides she might as well say hi, and heads over.

"Hey," she says as she sidles down the row.

"Hey," says Swapna. "You're a Hitchcock fan, too, huh? I guess that makes sense, since you like horror movies. I don't normally like slasher movies or any of that, but I mean, Hitchcock is like a whole different level, right?"

"Oh, I don't really know Hitchcock," admits Jinx as she settles into the seat next to her.

"How can you not know Hitchcock?" asks Swapna. "He's like one of the most famous filmmakers ever."

Jinx shrugs. "You said it's horror?"

"Well, *North by Northwest* is more suspense than horror, but Hitchcock did some proper horror movies, too, like *The Birds* and *Psycho*."

"Oh, I've heard of *Psycho*," says Jinx. "Norman Bates, right? Ran a hotel and stabbed his customers while they were in the shower?"

Swapna rolls her eyes. "I mean, technically, yeah, but it's way more than that. *Psycho* is a classic. I mean, *all* Hitchcock films are classics, I guess. But that's definitely a big one. Like, he pioneered so many film techniques that today we just kind of take for granted, you know?"

She seems a lot more excited to talk about film*making*

than she did about acting, which makes Jinx wonder something.

"You really get into movies, huh?"

Swapna looks embarrassed. "Yeah, I guess I'm like a film nerd or something."

"Would you rather *make* movies than act in them?"

The question seems to surprise Swapna. "Well, I mean . . . eventually, sure. But even if I don't really want to be an actor, I think it'll be a good experience because a director needs to be able to talk to her actors. It'll help if I have some acting experience myself."

"That makes sense," says Jinx. "I was honestly kind of confused about the whole acting thing because you've never talked about it before, but now I get it."

"Well, also my *mom* wants me to do it," says Swapna. "I think because she wishes that *she* was an actress."

"What's that got to do with you?" asks Jinx.

Swapna laughs. "Right? Ugh. It's like some weird mom thing, you know?"

"Not really."

Jinx didn't mean to say that. It just kind of slipped out. And she *definitely* didn't mean for it to sound so . . . *harsh*. But Swapna flinches a little, like it actually hurt.

"Sorry, I just—I wasn't thinking," she stammers.

It was an accident. Jinx knows that. People love to complain about their moms for some reason. Maybe because they can bond over it. Everybody has a mom, right? Well, except Jinx. She's never even met her mother. But she can't expect people to always remember that. This isn't the first time it's happened to her. In fact, she's lost count how many times. Once is whatever. A drop. But it keeps happening, over and over, with all different kinds of people. Each drip adds a little more, spreading out a bit further each time. Like dark ink on parchment.

Not that she can *tell* people that, of course. They'd either worry about her even more or decide they don't want to be around her. Probably both.

So she just says, "It's fine."

And she means it.

Or, well, she *wants* to mean it. That's what counts, right?

After that awkward exchange, they sit in uncomfortable silence, waiting for the suspense movie to begin.

15

THE LIBRARY

Jinx has a hard time getting into the movie. She doesn't really understand why it's called suspense when it's mostly just some adults standing around talking. She starts wishing she had her camera again. She wants to hold it. To look through it. To focus on it, not on this dull, black-and-white movie. She gets restless and fidgety, and she can tell that's bothering Swapna, who is trying to focus on the movie. So after a half hour or so, she gives up and quietly slips out of the theater.

As she walks through the lobby, Ms. Linkenholker asks, "Not feeling it, Jinx?"

Jinx doesn't want Ms. Linkenholker to think her movies are boring, so she says, "Oh, uh, it's great. I just remembered I need to do something."

"Okay, well, you're always welcome."

"Thanks, Ms. Linkenholker."

Of course the problem is, Jinx doesn't actually have something to do. So now what?

Well, she tried distracting herself from her camera problem, and that didn't work. Maybe, since she can't stop thinking about it anyway, she should learn more about it instead. And she knows that the best place to learn about stuff is the library.

The Greenbelt Public Library is pretty small, but it has a nice "Teen Zone" section with some tables and chairs surrounded on all sides by YA books. There's also a kids area that she used to love when she was little. Sometimes, she would show up for the reading times even when she was a little too old for them, just because she liked listening to the librarian's soothing voice. And before Blaine built her computer, she would often use the library computers to watch videos about photography and learn how to edit images.

Now she goes up to the information counter, where an older man with a beard sits typing on a computer.

"Good morning, Mr. Humphries."

He looks up, and his face brightens. "Jinx! Good morning! What can I do for you?"

"Do we have any books about spirit photography?"

"Oh, looking to learn some new creative techniques, huh?"

"Sure," she says, because she doesn't want to get into the real reason with him.

"Such an interesting trend, wasn't it?" he says as he begins searching on his computer. "I read somewhere that the reason seeing spirits became so popular was because of all the death and horror that people witnessed during World War I. They were looking for some kind of comforting, tangible assurance that their deceased loved ones were okay."

"I can understand that," Jinx says truthfully.

Mr. Humphries pauses a moment in his typing, and the *concerned* expression flashes across his face. Then he goes back to looking at the monitor, and his face brightens.

"Ah, here we are. It's called *The Perfect Medium: Photography and the Occult* by Clément Chéroux. It's in the photography section. Want me to write down the number for you?"

She shakes her head. "I know that section pretty well."

He smiles. "I'm sure you do."

Jinx goes back to the photography section, where she's spent a lot of time over the past couple of years. Her fingers slide gently across the spines as she searches for the book. Today her Band-Aids are yellow to match her T-shirt, which has the album cover for *Sailing the Seas of Cheese* by Primus on the front. The cover image is exactly what it sounds like: a Claymation-style picture of a pirate ship sailing through a yellow sea of cheese, with a shark, an octopus, and a bearded merman swimming around it.

She spots the heavy, hardbound photography book and takes it over to a table. Somebody at the library appreciates symmetrically placed seating, and she savors that for a moment. Then she slips into a chair and begins to read.

The book shows page after page of old-fashioned people posing with ghostly apparitions floating around them. The ghost is sometimes a child, other times an old person. One strangely meta image depicts a table with a framed photograph on it. And surrounding the table are four child spirits that seem like they could also be the children in the photo. Jinx gazes at it a long time, unsure exactly why she feels so drawn to it. Maybe it's like Mr. Humphries said. People who have seen horror and death want tangible proof that their loved one is okay.

For just a moment, Jinx imagines herself sitting on a stool in an empty white room. The light is soft. The floor is hardwood, like her home. Someone is taking her picture. She doesn't know who, because she can't see them. She's the camera looking at herself sitting on the stool. And behind her, pale and wavering like drifting smoke, is her father. A little heavyset, with spiky dark hair, a goatee, and silver hoop earrings. His expression should be too ghostly to discern. But she can. She can see it. The quiet, weary despair of a man who did not like his life, and ultimately decided to leave it.

This imaginary image was supposed to comfort her, like it comforted all those people long ago. But it doesn't. It sends a corkscrew of dread down into her. She can taste it, like a metallic tang on her tongue. She wraps her arms around her torso and squeezes as hard as she can, but it doesn't lessen the twisting pressure. She only knows one true escape from this feeling.

Jinx slaps the book closed loud enough that people look up. But then they see that it's her, and they all look *concerned* because *everyone knows* what happened, and that just makes it all worse. She keeps her eyes fixed to the floor as she hurries toward the front door.

"Jinx? You okay?" she hears Mr. Humphries ask, but she keeps going.

Why does everyone ask her that question? What makes them think she might be okay? What makes them think she will *ever* be okay? What makes them think she *deserves* to be okay?

16

THE ROCK STAR

Jinx staggers out of the library, fumbling for her phone. It's not her Canon 5D Mark III DSLR, but at least it takes pictures, so maybe it will relieve some of this pressure.

"I am a camera," she whispers as she presses the phone to her forehead. "That's all that I am."

She starts taking pictures. The flowers in front of the library, the memorial bench, people walking past, a ladybug on a leaf. It doesn't matter. The point is to put her focus *out there* rather than let it continue to twist within her chest. To make it about some *thing*, and not about her. And while she hates the phone's photo settings, the meager heft, and the lack of a proper viewfinder, taking pictures with it *does* make her feel a little more at ease—a little less like the world is crumbling beneath her feet.

Once she's feeling better, she sits on the steps of the Community Center Building to collect herself. Out of idle curiosity, she decides to check if anything she took is halfway decent. But then her breath catches in her throat.

The most recent image shows the community center, which has a bas-relief sculpture depicting all different kinds of workers, united, marching in a line. But something is wrong with them. Instead of looking noble and proud like normal, in this picture their eyes are narrow and smeared with soot. Their mouths are also blackened, and curled into sneers.

And hovering above them is the specter.

Jinx stares incredulously at the image. She closes her eyes and opens them again.

It's all still there.

She flips to another image. It's a picture of a bird sitting in the thick branches of one of Greenbelt's largest, oldest trees. But now, obscuring the bird is the specter, perched on the branch like a giant, murky raven. Thin black tendrils snake down from the branch, reaching forward, toward the camera, toward her . . .

Jinx lurches up from the bench as if she can feel those tendrils touching her feet. That's not possible of course. They aren't really there. She looks down to make sure and doesn't see them. But she can still *feel* them coming for her.

She stumbles across the wide grass lawn in front of the library. She imagines them snapping at her heels, threading, groping, wanting to pull her down. The twisting in her stomach is worse. So much worse. Like something is pressing on her insides. Like something wants to escape.

Why is this still happening to her? She wasn't even using the camera. It doesn't make sense because it's the *camera* that's haunted, right?

Wrong.

Now she understands. Now she finally gets it. The camera isn't haunted.

She is.

Jinx jerks to a sudden stop in the middle of the lawn. She stares up into the blue skies above, directly at the sun. It blinds her, makes her unable to see this thing that's coming for her. Despite the heat of the day and the sweat soaking into her hair, her skin feels cold and clammy. Her brain is a mess of static and endlessly looping questions: Why is this happening? What should she do? What *can* she do? If it's not a problem with the camera, then it's a problem with *her*. And if *she's* the problem, then there is no escape. No release from this horrible, awful feeling.

No escape . . . except . . . except—

"Jinx!"

Monica's voice splashes into the noise in her brain like a rescue float. Jinx blinks, her vision now filled with spots from staring into the sun. She looks around as her heart slows, the dark spots fade, and the world gradually stabilizes into something that at least *appears* to make sense.

Monica is stretched out on a blanket at the edge of the lawn, under the shade of a tree. Seth sits next to her, the remnants of a picnic lunch between them. They're both dressed in regular shorts and T-shirts now. Monica props herself up on her elbow as she smiles and beckons Jinx over with one slim brown arm.

Not knowing what else to do, Jinx walks over to them.

"Hang with us a bit." Monica pats the blanket beside her.

Jinx obediently sits.

"What's going on, Jinxie?" Monica's tone is cheerful, but it's clear by her serious brown eyes that this is not an idle question. "Talk to me."

"I was kinda freaking out a little," admits Jinx.

"Yeah, looked like it," says Monica. "You want to talk about it?"

Jinx glances at Seth, who's staring at his phone, then

shakes her head. She doesn't have anything against him, but she also doesn't know him very well.

Monica catches this, then nods. "Take a rain check on that. Anyway, those new shots you took the other day were great."

"Oh, thanks." Jinx tries to sound grateful, but it comes out a little forced.

Monica nudges Seth. "Weren't her photos great?"

Seth tears himself away from whatever he was looking at with obvious effort, but after a moment to adjust, he nods emphatically. "Yeah, even better than the last set. Honestly, I can't believe you're self-taught."

"I took a beginner course at the community center." Jinx points to the building behind them with her chin.

"Okay, but yours look *professional*. Seriously."

Jinx blushes and begins plucking at the grass as she talks. "So I, uh, watched the show a couple nights ago. *Battle Maidens.*"

"Really?" Monica looks genuinely surprised.

"What'd you think?" asks Seth.

"It's . . . a lot," says Jinx. "Probably should have started with season one."

Monica laughs. "Yeah, you should have."

"Starting with the latest season?" Seth looks almost admiring. "That must have been *so* confusing."

"Yeah . . ." says Jinx.

"Oh!" Monica claps her hands together, her eyebrows jumping. "We should totally have a re-watch party with Jinx!"

"Hey, yeah! Tia was just saying we should do a re-watch binge before the final episode of the season," agrees Seth. "And it's always more fun to have someone who's never seen it."

"We could do it at my parents' house," says Monica. "Plenty of room for all of us, *and* it's right down the street from Jinx's aunt's house. We'll make snacks and turn it into a thing!"

"I like this plan!" says Seth.

Monica turns to Jinx. "What do you say? Up for it?"

Jinx can't quite convince herself that four grad students would really want to hang out with a middle schooler, but obviously she's not going to call them out on it. So instead, she shrugs.

"Sure, that'd be fun."

She doesn't know if binge-watching a frenetic show like *Battle Maidens: Extreme Metal Squad* would be fun. But she thinks hanging out with the four of them would be. Plus, there's no way Blaine can still treat her like a kid once he learns that she's hanging out with people even older than him.

"Hi, Jinx!" Ms. Linkenholker waves as she walks past their blanket, headed toward the library.

"Hey, Ms. Linkenholker." Jinx politely waves back.

Once Ms. Linkenholker is out of earshot, Seth turns to Jinx. "Okay, is it just me or do you know literally everyone in Greenbelt?"

"I guess because I grew up here," she says.

"*I* grew up here, too, and I don't know *half* the people you do," points out Monica.

"Right?" says Seth. "How come you're basically a local celebrity?"

Monica gives him an incredulous smile. "Um, hello, because she's *Jinx?*"

"Sure, that's fair," says Seth. "Don't get me wrong, Jinx. You are way cooler than any twelve-year-old has a right to be. I was just wondering, like, how did the Jinx fan club start?"

Jinx isn't comfortable with the direction of this conversation. If it were Blaine, she would tell him to shut up. But Blaine wouldn't talk about it in the first place. She goes back to picking at the grass, carefully tying one thin blade to the next with a teeny little square knot.

"Hmm." Monica frowns thoughtfully as she considers Seth's question. "I guess it started because her dad was like a super-famous rock star? And then . . ." She trails off as she realizes where the conversation is inevitably going.

But Seth doesn't know. Yet. "Jinx, your dad was a *rock star*? I had no idea! What band was he in? What did he play?"

"He was the lead singer of In-Sufferable," Jinx says, her eyes firmly fixed on her rapidly expanding grass chain.

"Oh man, I remember them!" says Seth, still not getting it. "They had that big song, right? What was it . . . 'The Suns of Other Worlds'!"

"Yeah," Jinx says tonelessly.

"Geez, I think I even remember some of the words . . ."

"Uh, Seth . . ." Monica says uneasily.

"Hang on," Seth waves her away, now completely focused on recall. "That song was totally my jam for a while. I think it went something like 'I look at the stars in the sky, at the suns of other worlds, and I wonder when I die, will they still'—ouch!"

He looks in confusion at Monica, who has just pinched his arm. Then he looks at Jinx as she steadfastly continues her grass chain. Then his mouth opens in an O shape.

Now he gets it.

"Jinx, I'm so sorry. I forgot that he . . ." His face blanches. "And you . . ."

"It's fine, don't worry about it," Jinx says in a monotone. "I have to go."

"Wait, Jinx—" begins Monica.

But Jinx is already gone.

17

THE BOILING POT

Jinx has a memory from when she was little. Maybe four or five? It isn't her worst memory, of course. But it does come back to her now and then.

In this memory, she stood in the cramped, narrow kitchen in her old house. Her father was making her mac and cheese on the stove. He wore a Frank Black T-shirt. It was black with purple, all-capital letters that read: FRNK BLCK. He'd gained more weight over the last few years, so the shirt was stretched tightly across his stomach. But he wouldn't stop wearing it because he loved that shirt.

Jinx was short enough back then that her face was about

even with the pot that sat on the stove. She watched the heat coil gradually turn bright orange, and waited for the covered pot to begin boiling.

"A watched pot never boils, Jinxie." Her father stood beside her at the counter as he measured out the milk and butter that would be mixed in with the cheese powder, which was at least as brightly orange as the heat coil.

"Why not?" she asked.

He smiled as he continued to work. "It's just a saying. It means the more you focus on waiting for something, the longer it'll seem to take. But if you go do something else, it'll be done before you know it."

"Oh," said Jinx, but she didn't take her eyes off the pot.

Her father moved back and forth along their narrow kitchen, from the sink to the counter and back, crossing behind her each time. The pot lid was glass, so she could see the steam begin to collect underneath. It wasn't boiling yet, but it was getting closer.

"You're kind of in the way," her father said as he

shuffled past, his firm belly grazing the back of her head.

"Sorry," she mumbled, but didn't think to move.

The lid began to tremble as the steam built up within the pot. Little puffs spurted out now and then, relieving some of the pressure, but never for long. Then at last the pot truly began to boil, and the lid rattled loudly.

"Daddy, it's ready."

She pointed to the pot.

He turned, and his expression became panicked.

"Don't touch it!"

She hadn't been about to touch it. She wasn't *dumb*. But he smacked her hand away, hard enough to sting. When he did this, he accidentally jostled the pot handle, and boiling water splashed onto his hand.

"Ah!" he yelled loudly, then cursed. He pushed roughly past her to get to the sink. "I told you to get out of the way!"

Had he told her to get out of the way? She didn't remember that. He'd said she was *in* the way. She should have realized that meant she should move. But she didn't. Maybe she was dumb after all.

He continued to mutter curses as he ran his hand under cold water from the sink. She watched him, feeling like it was her fault, because she had been in his way.

She was *always* in his way.

18

THE CAMERA OBSCURA

That afternoon, Jinx and Blaine head back to George's Cameras.

On the drive over, Blaine asks, "Did George say he fixed it?"

"No," says Jinx. "There's nothing wrong with it."

"What about the glitch?"

Once Jinx had time to think about it calmly, everything made sense. The camera was never haunted. It's just a tool to help her see what—or rather, *who* is coming.

For her.

She can't tell Blaine that, of course. He probably wouldn't

believe her. And if he did, then he'd be worried for her. She doesn't want to him worry. He doesn't *need* to worry. Not like her.

"Don't worry about it," she tells him.

Blaine looks at her a moment, like he can tell she's holding back. But, thankfully, he doesn't push, and they drive the rest of the way to the camera shop in silence. Jinx hopes he'll let it go completely, but once he parks the car, he tries again.

"Jinx, what you said yesterday . . . about wronging your dad or whatever . . ."

She stays silent, her eyes fixed forward, even though the car is parked and the only thing to look at is the GEORGE'S CAMERAS sign over the shop. Sometimes she wishes Blaine didn't understand her so well.

"You know that's not true, right?" he presses.

Her neck is tense with the effort of keeping her face forward. She can feel the headache creeping in. But Blaine doesn't let up.

"Jinx, what happened wasn't your fault."

There it is. And when she hears it, it takes *effort* not to grimace. She understands why he says it. Because he doesn't know any better. She's never told him—or anyone—what her father said to her on the day he died. Or what she said after.

"Can you wait in the car?" she asks.

Blaine stares at her. "Are you serious?"

"Yeah."

"But . . ." He's really struggling now. Jinx feels bad about that. He's normally the most easygoing person in the world, but maybe everyone has their limits.

"Sorry," she says. "I promise I'll make it up to you."

"What? No, that's not . . ." Blaine isn't the most eloquent guy, and he doesn't seem to know how to say what he's feeling. Jinx can relate to that.

"Please, Blaine?"

He closes his eyes and takes a deep breath.

"Yeah, okay. I'll wait here."

"Thank you." She opens the car door and quickly exits before he changes his mind.

When she enters the store, she finds George sealing up a small rectangular cardboard box with black electrical tape. He's so focused on it that he doesn't seem to notice her arrival.

"What are you doing?" she asks.

He looks up and grins. "This, my fellow photographer, is a miracle."

When she hears the phrase "my fellow photographer," it's like a comforting blanket falls over her. The tension in her neck recedes, and the nearly unbearable pressure on her chest lessens. She is *always* ready to talk photography.

"What is it?" She drifts over for a closer look.

"Hang on, not done just yet."

At one end of the rectangle, he cuts a small hole on the left side and a tiny puncture on the right side. Then he holds up the box so one eye is looking into the larger hole.

"It's a camera obscura!" he declares.

She isn't sure if he's joking. "That's . . . a camera?"

"The very *first* type of camera, in fact." He hands her the box, then hurries over to his bookshelves. "The phrase 'camera obscura' is Latin," George continues. "It means 'dark chamber.' Way back before what we call cameras were invented, people discovered that if you have a totally dark room with just one tiny hole that lets in light from outside, the little bit of light will project whatever is outside the room. Like a tree or a building or whatever."

He pulls out a book and flips through it until he finds an illustration of a tree and a room. Lines from the tree converge on a tiny hole in the outer wall of the room, then expand inside to project a smaller, upside-down version of the tree on the far inside wall.

George taps the illustration with his finger and smiles at her. "Make sense?"

"And this . . ." She looks down at the box in her hands. "It's like a miniature room?"

"Exactly! Go stand with your back to the window."

As she positions herself in front of the window, he puts the book back on the shelf, then hurries over to the light switch by the door.

"It'll be easier to see if I turn out the lights."

He flicks off the lights, but they aren't in total darkness because sunlight is coming through the windows.

"Now hold up the box and look into the larger hole," he says. "Just make sure your head isn't blocking the smaller hole."

Jinx looks into the box. She can see Blaine's car. It's blurry and upside down, but it's a real projection.

"So . . . what's inside the box?"

"A sheet of plain white paper," George says.

"That's it?"

"That's all it needs. Physics takes care of the rest! Of course, if we put a lens over the pinhole, that would sharpen the image. And if we put a mirror inside the box, that would flip the image so it looked right side up."

"Just like a camera." She lowers the camera obscura and gazes down at it.

"This is basically the modern camera's great-grandaddy," says George. "It all started with something like this."

"Camera obscura . . ." She slowly turns it in her hands. Such a simple thing. It really does feel like magic. "The dark chamber."

"Pretty neat, right?" George asks.

"Yeah."

He flicks the lights back on. "You keep it."

"You sure?"

He rolls his eyes. "I have plenty of boxes, tape, and paper. Consider it an apology present."

"Apology?" All her wonder evaporates, and the rods of tension are back. "Did something happen to my camera?"

"Nothing happened to your camera," he says quickly. "In fact, that's the point. I have no idea how or why it was glitching, and I couldn't get it to glitch for me. I couldn't find *anything* wrong with it."

"Oh." Some, but not all, of her tension eases. She looks back down at her camera obscura. "You know that guy who used to take spirit photographs?"

"Mumler, you mean?"

"Yeah. Did he say he did it with a special camera?"

George shakes his head. "Mumler claimed it wasn't the camera, it was him. That he was like somehow in tune with the spirit realm or something, and the camera was just the way he channeled it."

"So it would work with any camera?"

"I guess," says George. "I mean, if we're pretending for a moment that any of it was real."

"Right," Jinx says. "But it's not."

"Of course not."

"Of course not," repeats Jinx in a hollow voice.

He gazes at her a moment, his expression solemn. "I feel like I'm missing something here."

"Yeah." A part of her wants to show him the images on her phone. George seems nice. And he might even have a better idea of what's going on if he knows it's showing up on other cameras. Or maybe he'd decide she's creepy, or messing with him. She doesn't know him well enough to predict that. So she keeps it to herself. "Can I have my camera back?"

"Of course!" He hurries behind the counter and pulls out her camera bag. "Here you go, fully inspected, free of charge."

"Thanks." She opens the bag and examines the camera and lens. Everything looks perfect.

"Did you think I was going to hand you back a smudged lens or something?" He sounds mildly insulted.

She gives him a tiny smile and shakes her head. "Thanks again, George. I better go. My friend is waiting."

19

THE DARK CHAMBER

Jinx climbs back into the car, her camera bag over one shoulder, her camera obscura tucked under her arm. Blaine looks at her expectantly.

"My camera's fine," she tells him.

"Just like you predicted."

"Yeah."

"And you knew because . . ."

She looks down at the camera obscura in her lap and shrugs.

He doesn't start the car, so they just sit there.

Finally he asks, "You're really not going to tell me how you knew?"

She shakes her head.

Blaine gives an exasperated sigh as he starts up the car. "Sometimes you're like talking into a black hole. Things go in, but nothing ever comes out."

"Sorry."

"You don't need to apologize." He pulls out of the parking lot and starts driving back toward Greenbelt. "But it would be nice to know what's going on inside that black box you have for a brain."

"A dark chamber," she says.

"Sure, or that."

She feels bad. She doesn't like keeping stuff from him. But what can she say? Does she tell him about the phone? That the smudge is basically inescapable? That she's cursed? Or haunted? Maybe even *hunted*? Does she tell him how she feels this slow dread creeping over her, bit by bit, growing each time she sees that the specter is a little closer? And she suspects it's getting *stronger*, too, the way it's begun to warp the stuff around it in photos. Like it's infecting the world with its malice. Does she tell him that whatever or whoever is coming for her . . . maybe she deserves it?

No, she can't say any of that to Blaine. It would freak him out. He'd tell her aunt that he's really worried about her. Then her aunt would freak out and do who knows what. Have Jinx committed maybe? And Blaine would feel terrible about that. Jinx doesn't want Blaine to feel terrible about anything. Especially not about her.

So instead she tells him, "Thanks for being such a good friend."

He gives her a rueful smile. "And then you go and say something like that. How could I possibly stay mad at you?"

Blaine drops her off at home. It's still midafternoon, so Aunt Helen hasn't left for work yet. When Jinx walks through the front door, her aunt is in the kitchen packing a lunch for herself.

"Hey, Auntie." Jinx hurries past her toward the stairs.

"Wait." Firm, parental voice.

Jinx freezes. It's not a tone Aunt Helen takes very often.

"Yeah?"

Her aunt walks over to the couch and sits down, then pats the spot next to her.

"Come sit with me."

"Okay . . ." Jinx reluctantly walks over.

"You're not in trouble," her aunt assures her.

Jinx isn't sure about that but nods anyway.

"I got a call from Mr. Humphries at the library."

Jinx doesn't know what to make of this, and stays silent.

"And then I got a text from Monica," says Aunt Helen.

Jinx is starting to understand where this is going. But she still stays silent.

"They both—*separately*—asked me if you were okay. They each said you seemed like you were kind of struggling today."

Jinx looks down at her camera obscura. She wishes her

head *was* a black box or dark chamber that could contain all her feelings forever. Especially the thick, seething ones now rising in her gorge.

"*Are* you okay?" presses Aunt Helen.

Jinx stays quiet. She just has to keep it all contained. That's it.

Aunt Helen also stays quiet.

They sit there for several moments. It's clear her aunt wants something from her. She doesn't know what that is, or if she can give it to her. But she knows she has to say something.

"I'm trying really hard."

Aunt Helen looks at her a moment, then pulls her in close.

"Kiddo, being okay isn't something you should have to work at. It shouldn't take a huge amount of effort simply to feel okay."

"I know."

A pause.

"Do you want to talk about it?"

"No."

Another pause.

"Would you talk to Ms. Simmons about it?"

"Maybe."

"I called her a little while ago. She had a cancellation, so there was an opening tomorrow morning. I already booked it."

"Oh."

"Sorry if that's sudden," says her aunt. "But, I just . . ." Her face tenses. Jinx can really see that strain right now. The effort it takes her aunt to be okay, too. "After what happened to your dad, I just . . ." Her voice cracks. "I can't lose you, too."

She squeezes Jinx harder, then she closes her eyes as tears roll down her cheeks.

It hurts Jinx to watch her aunt cry. It's an actual pain in her chest, like a fist gripping her heart.

"I'm sorry, Auntie."

"Baby . . ." Her aunt kisses the top of her head. "You have nothing to be sorry about. *Nothing*, understand?"

Jinx says, "Sure."

Not because she believes that, but because she knows it will make her aunt feel a little better if she agrees.

After a few moments, Aunt Helen takes a big, sniffly breath and smiles with some additional effort. "We'll be okay."

"Yep," says Jinx, again because she knows it's what her aunt wants to hear.

"I have to go to work, kiddo. Get a good night's sleep so you'll be fresh for your appointment tomorrow."

"I'll try," promises Jinx.

Once her aunt is gone, she takes an extra-long time resetting the house. That helps a little. Then she heads up to her bedroom. But once she's there, she isn't sure what to do. She still feels that heavy dread. It sits in her chest like a belligerent stone gargoyle. Is the specter really her father coming to punish her for ruining his life? Is there any escape from it? Should she even want to escape? Maybe it's what she deserves. But then she thinks of those sneering, dark-eyed workers, the hazy black raven with its inky tendrils reaching for her, and she doesn't care if she deserves it or not. She just wants to get *away* from it. But how? What can she do?

Jinx paces back and forth in her tiny room, shaking her hands helplessly, desperately wanting to dispel the pressure building inside her. But she doesn't want to take pictures. She doesn't want to see the specter getting a little closer with each shot, or making the world look even worse than it already is. Maybe if she never takes another picture ever again, it won't get any closer or stronger. Can she even do that?

The camera obscura sits on her desk. Jinx gazes thoughtfully at it for a moment. It doesn't actually take pictures, but maybe that's better. At least for right now.

She picks it up and presses it to her forehead. "I am a camera. That's all that I am."

Then she turns her back to the window and looks through the hole into the tiny dark chamber.

There is the tall tree leaning behind her house, blurry and upside down.

And there is the specter.

Except, unlike the tree, the specter is still somehow right side up. And it's noticeably closer than even that morning at the library. She can see its dark, murky edges unfurl slowly, like ink spreading across a pool of water. It happens so gradually that at first she doesn't understand what she's looking at. And then all at once she does.

Jinx is watching it move.

20
THE TEST

Tappity-tappity. Tap. Tap. Tappity-tappity. Tap. Tap.

Pause.

Tappity-tappity. Tap. Tap. Tappity-tappity. Tap. Tap.

"What's the holdup, kiddo?" asks Aunt Helen.

Jinx stands at the front door, her hand on the knob. Her back is turned so her aunt can't see that she's been tapping her special sequence on the knob over and over again. It's supposed to make her feel better. It's supposed to get rid of the feeling that when she leaves the house, she'll come back to horror. Why does it usually work? No idea.

But this morning, it doesn't.

Her fingertips are covered in glittery princess Band-Aids to match her T-shirt, which has the cover for the album *Live Through This* by Hole. The image shows a demented-looking prom queen with wild eyes and smeared makeup. Jinx taps her prom queen sparkly fingers on the doorknob in the same pattern she's used every day, multiple times a day, for the last year. But for the first time ever, it doesn't make her feel better.

She didn't sleep well last night. Every time she closed her eyes, she saw that dark shape slowly spreading across her vision like some spectral disease seeping into her brain. She almost destroyed her camera obscura after she realized it was able to show her the spirit's movements in real time. But then she realized that might be a terrible mistake. She'd first assumed it moved only when she was taking pictures of it. Now she understands that it is moving *regardless* of what she does. Having a tool that allows her to monitor its progress is scary but maybe also necessary for her survival.

The real question now is what will happen once it

reaches her. If it truly is her father, will he be mad? Will he punish her for ruining his life? After all, what other reason would he have for haunting her?

"Okay, Jinx, we really have to go now or we'll be late."

Aunt Helen steps around her and opens the door without even an "Allons-y!" When Jinx sees it swing open before she's ready, a spike of alarm shoots through her chest and she lets out an involuntary gasp. Her aunt continues down the walkway toward the parking lot, but stops and looks back. Jinx is still standing in the doorway.

"Come on, kiddo." She gestures impatiently. "I know you're nervous about talking to Ms. Simmons, but we need to move."

Jinx wasn't even thinking about Ms. Simmons yet. Now it adds a whole new layer of pressure. She wants to close the door and start over. She wants to do that really badly. But then her aunt will want to know why she's doing that, and the idea of explaining sounds even worse. So with clenched jaw and shaky steps, she forces herself to walk to the car and climb into the passenger side.

Her mind is such a blur of anxiety that she barely notices the drive. The next thing she knows, they've arrived at the medical office complex. She follows her aunt past signs for a dentist, an orthopedist, and a physical therapy facility, until they arrive at the door marked KIMBERLY SIMMONS, LCSW.

Jinx always finds the waiting room somewhat soothing. It's just a couch, a couple of soft chairs, and a coffee table with mental health magazines spread neatly across it like giant playing cards, everything orderly and symmetrical. The room is filled with a quiet hiss from the white-noise machine that sits in the corner and prevents people from overhearing whatever is said behind the closed door.

She and her aunt sit on the couch to wait. A short time later, a teenager in a long gray overcoat comes out of Ms. Simmons's office, hands deep in their pockets, eyes fixed firmly to the ground as they hurry past and out the exit.

A few minutes later, Ms. Simmons steps into the open doorway.

"Jinx? You ready?"

Jinx wants to say no. Can she say no? Maybe, but not in front of Aunt Helen. So she says nothing and hurries into the room, closing the door firmly behind her. Then she turns around. And the hairs on the back of her neck stand on end.

Something is deeply wrong with the room.

"Jinx?" Ms. Simmons sits calmly in her chair as if everything is fine even though *nothing* is fine. "Won't you sit?"

"Uh . . ." That's as much as she can get out. After that, she just continues to stand there, wondering how angry her aunt would be if she simply turned around and left.

They remain like that for several moments, Jinx struggling not to freak out, Ms. Simmons smiling at her as though the room is exactly the way it always is. Does she not realize? Can't she tell how messed up it is?

Finally, Ms. Simmons says, "I moved some things around."

"Yeah," says Jinx.

"I thought you might notice. Can you tell me which ones?"

Jinx points to the candle on the bookshelf, which is no longer centered in the space, then at the frog figurine on the side table that is tilted at an odd angle. Finally, she points at Ms. Simmons's chair, which is no longer perpendicular to Jinx's chair.

Ms. Simmons nods. "That's right. Normally, I keep everything very symmetrical because it gives some of my clients a sense of calm."

Jinx nods. She is clearly one of those clients.

"But sometimes it's good to challenge things," continues Ms. Simmons. "Although I have to admit, this is hitting you harder than I thought it would. I was hoping we could get through the session like this, but looking at you now, I think that would be pretty tough."

"Yeah," agrees Jinx.

"Would you like me to fix everything?"

Jinx nods again.

Without another word, Ms. Simmons stands, then moves everything back where it's supposed to go. She sits down again and smiles.

"Won't you please sit?"

Jinx is still pretty rattled, but she manages to cross the room and sit in her chair.

"Jinx, have you ever heard of obsessive-compulsive disorder, or OCD?"

"That's where people wash their hands until they bleed, right?"

"That is one way it can manifest," agrees Ms. Simmons. "But it can appear in all sorts of ways. Like the name suggests, there are two parts of OCD. First there is the obsession, which is usually an upsetting thought or feeling that keeps coming back again and again, no matter how hard the person tries not to think about it. And then there is the compulsion, which is usually an action the person takes to temporarily chase the unpleasant thought or feeling away. The two don't have to be logically connected in any way, but when you do the action, the obsession goes away for a little while."

"So you think I have OCD?"

"Most people don't get quite so upset because I've changed the angle of my chair."

Jinx wants to say that it's not normally this bad. She's just had a rough couple of days. But then she'd have to tell Ms. Simmons *why* it's been a rough couple of days, and she's pretty sure that telling your therapist you're scared that your father's spirit is coming to wreak vengeance on you is a great way to get locked up somewhere. So instead, she just says, "Sorry."

"It's nothing to be sorry about," says Ms. Simmons. "But it *is* something we should take seriously. Left untreated, OCD can cause you real harm. It can take over your entire life and lead to all sorts of unhealthy, and even dangerous, behaviors."

"I just like things to be neat," says Jinx.

"Lots of people do, and there's nothing wrong with that," says Ms. Simmons. "But a person who does not have OCD could sit down in that chair and have a conversation with me while all those things were out of place, even if they didn't like it. You, it seems, could not."

"So it was a test?"

"I'd call it more of an assessment," says Ms. Simmons.

Jinx isn't sure she sees much difference, but there's something more important she wants to ask.

"Why am I like this?"

"We don't completely know what causes OCD yet," admits Ms. Simmons. "Research seems to suggest there may be a genetic component."

"You mean I inherited it? But my dad wasn't like this." He was actually an even worse slob than Aunt Helen.

"Maybe your mom was," says Ms. Simmons.

"Oh." Jinx hadn't thought of that. She hardly ever thinks about her mom. Probably because Janice McCormick died while giving birth to her. Jinx has never met her because she accidentally killed her by being born.

"It's not *just* caused by genetics," Ms. Simmons continues. "There are other factors that can contribute to the development of OCD as well. One of those factors can be a traumatic life event, like the one you experienced."

Jinx has always liked things to be neat and tidy. Did it get more intense after her father died? She can't quite remember what it was like before and doesn't want to talk about that anyway, so she changes the subject. "Is there a cure?"

Ms. Simmons considers a moment. "I'm not sure *cure* is the right word. Like I said, there's nothing wrong with enjoying cleanliness and organization. The important thing is to make sure it doesn't control your life. There are two treatments that can be used together or separately, which studies have shown really help. One is medication. The other is something called Exposure and Response Prevention, or ERP."

"What is that?" Whatever it is, Jinx thinks it sounds painful.

"All right, so stay with me for a minute on this," says Ms. Simmons. "A home alarm system is supposed to warn you if there's an intruder breaking into your home, right? But what if the alarm system malfunctions and mistakes your cat for an intruder? You'd hear the alarm and think you were in danger, even though you really weren't."

"Okay . . ." Jinx isn't sure where this is going.

"Now, think of fear as sort of like your *body's* alarm system. It warns you when there's danger, and that keeps you safe. But let's imagine that OCD is when your body's alarm system malfunctions. A crooked chair isn't actually dangerous, and your brain knows that. But your body sends the alarm anyway, and that's why it makes you *feel* so anxious."

"I guess that makes sense," says Jinx. "But what does that have to do with the exposure prevention thing?"

"Exposure and *Response* Prevention," says Ms. Simmons. "That part is really important. Basically we'll need to retune your alarm system so it stops malfunctioning and only alerts you when there's actual danger. The 'exposure' part is the obsessiveness. The upsetting thoughts or feelings that keep coming back. We're going to face them together, you and I, and rather than give in to the compulsion, we're going to find other ways to deal with it. In other words, we're going to face those fears again and again so that slowly, over time, your body learns that it's not actually dangerous."

"That sounds awful," says Jinx.

"It won't be easy," admits Ms. Simmons. "But . . . hmm, okay, maybe think about it like this. You ever watch monster movies?"

"Sure."

"Have you ever noticed that the scariest part is *before* you actually see the monster? Once you finally get a good look at it, it might be gross or creepy, but it's not nearly as scary as when it was lurking in the shadows."

"I guess that's true," says Jinx.

"Fear is always like that," says Ms. Simmons. "No matter how bad something really is, it's rarely as terrible as the thing we've conjured up in our imagination. A lot of times, when we finally gather our courage and open the door to face our fear, we find there's not even anything there."

Jinx thinks about the specter. It's hard to believe that it's nothing, especially since other people like Blaine and George are able to see it. But what if it really is her father, and he's not mad at her anymore? Is it possible that all the creepiness is something he can't help doing because he's dead, and dead-people stuff is just inherently creepy? Maybe he's actually coming back to say he *forgives* her for ruining his life.

That might actually feel pretty great.

"Okay," Jinx says. "Let's try it."

21

THE GIRL

After Jinx's session, Aunt Helen decides to take her out to lunch as a special treat.

"I'd say we've *both* earned it, kiddo," her aunt declares as they climb into the car. "Where do you want to go?"

"Franklin's," Jinx says promptly.

Aunt Helen smiles and shakes her head. "More pizza?"

"They have special pizza," says Jinx, which is true. She's not sure exactly what makes it special, but no other pizza tastes like Franklin's. And it's all the way over in Hyattsville, so she doesn't get to eat there very often. But

Ms. Simmons's office is already in College Park, so it's really only one more town over from where they are.

"They have great beer, too," says Aunt Helen. "Okay, let's do it."

Hyattsville has an arts district on Baltimore Avenue with all kinds of restaurants and shops, as well as some art galleries and a recording studio, which is why it's called the arts district. It also has a bunch of apartment buildings and town houses, although they all look sleek and modern. Jinx loves Greenbelt, of course, but if she was able to choose, she thinks she'd prefer one of the new-looking homes over something that purposefully looks the same as it did in 1937.

Franklin's is a two-story restaurant with lots of booths and bright colors. It has fun decorations, like a giant hand you can sit on while you're waiting for a table. It also has a general store attached, with lots of weird, kooky stuff for sale. But it's such an aggressively chaotic little shop that it kind of drives Jinx crazy to even go inside. She usually steers clear of it. The back wall of the restaurant is glass so people can see the big metal vats they use to brew beer. Jinx supposes that's why Aunt Helen likes their beer so much. It's made right there, so it must be really fresh or something. Jinx thinks beer smells horrible, but her dad used to drink it all the time, so she's used to it.

They're seated at a window booth near the entrance. Aunt Helen gets a burger, and Jinx gets a white pizza with extra cheese and bacon.

"You've basically ordered a heart attack on a plate," her aunt says.

Jinx shrugs. "Like you said, I should enjoy it now before I become a lacky."

Aunt Helen's eyes narrow. "*Lacky*? Are you . . . making fun of my lactose intolerance?"

"Maybe?" says Jinx, then flashes her a brief smile.

Her aunt gazes at her a moment. "I guess your session went pretty well? You seem to be in a better mood."

Jinx nods. "Ms. Simmons told you I probably have OCD?"

"Yeah, but we didn't talk about anything specific," she says. "Ms. Simmons respects your privacy. It's just, this is something I need to know about."

"I figured."

"How do you feel about it?"

Jinx considers a moment as she carefully tears off the corners of her paper place mat. "I guess a little relieved? Like, at least we know what's going on, and there's a way to deal with it."

"That's a great attitude, kiddo. I'm proud of you."

"Thanks." It still feels a little weird when her aunt says stuff like that, but it's not bad, exactly. Maybe she can get used to it.

"Ms. Simmons also told me that, at least for now, she wants you coming a couple times a week."

"But that'll be so expensive," says Jinx.

"Why are you always so worried about stuff like that?" Aunt Helen asks in exasperation. "When have I ever complained to you about money? Trust me, we are fine."

Jinx is considering whether to say that, in fact, Aunt Helen complains about money on a regular basis. But then she sees something that makes her forget everything else.

On the other side of the restaurant, in a small booth, sits Blaine. Across from him is *some girl* Jinx has never seen before. This girl is basically Jinx's worst nightmare. Her fingernails are painted in random colors with no discernible pattern. She's wearing a T-shirt with an extra-wide neck so it falls off one shoulder but not the other. She has short, punky blue hair that *could* have been fun, except the bangs are *crooked*. It's like this girl has gone out of her way to be *purposefully asymmetrical*. Jinx can't understand how Blaine can even *look* at her.

Aunt Helen follows Jinx's gaze over to the booth.

"Oh, that must be Blaine's new girlfriend. Don't they make a cute couple?"

Jinx stares at her aunt. "*Girlfriend?*"

"You haven't met her yet?" she asks in surprise.

"No," Jinx says quietly.

"Huh. I would have thought you'd be one of the first people he would introduce."

"I didn't even know he *had* a girlfriend." She tries to keep the hurt out of her voice, but clearly she fails, because her aunt suddenly looks pained.

"Oh, kiddo, I'm sorry. It's . . . look, this is complicated stuff. You know you're super important to him. Maybe he just . . ." She looks at Jinx helplessly.

"Maybe I would embarrass him," finishes Jinx.

"He's *not* embarrassed by you. You're like the coolest kid ever. It's just, well . . . you *are* still a kid."

Jinx realizes this was probably what he was talking about when he said he had to do "teenager stuff." He was going on a *date* with *asymmetry girl*.

Aunt Helen gives Jinx a thoughtful look. "He might have also been worried you'd get a little jealous. And judging by your reaction, maybe he's right."

Her eyes widen. "Me? Jealous of . . . *whoever* that is? No way."

"If you say so," replies Aunt Helen in a way that suggests she's not buying it.

Jinx's pizza arrives, but it's hard for her to fully enjoy it. She keeps glancing over at Blaine and his new girlfriend. The girl laughs too much. It's not like Blaine is a particularly funny guy, so she's clearly faking it so he'll like her more. Jinx would never fake that kind of stuff. Not that there's any point in comparing herself to this person, whoever they are. *Maybe* the girl would be kind of pretty if she didn't have those horrible bangs, but whatever. She'll never be as close to Blaine as Jinx.

Her aunt reaches across the table and pats her hand. "Growing up sucks, no matter what."

"What's that got to do with anything?" demands Jinx.

Aunt Helen just looks at her with a sad smile, then sighs. "You'll understand when you're a little older."

This does not make Jinx feel any better, and she picks at her pizza gloomily while her aunt finishes her burger and beer. She really hopes they can leave before

Blaine and the girlfriend notice them. Unfortunately, Aunt Helen is still sipping leisurely on her beer when Blaine and the girlfriend get up from their booth and head toward the door.

"We should say hi," murmurs Aunt Helen.

"What? No way!" hisses Jinx, her eyes fixed on her half-eaten pizza.

"It would be weird not to."

"Maybe he won't notice us."

"They literally have to walk past our booth."

"It's not like Blaine is super observant."

Aunt Helen just gives her another sad, knowing smile.

And almost as if he's trying to prove Jinx wrong, she hears Blaine's voice. "Oh, hey, guys."

"Hi, Blaine," Aunt Helen says cheerfully. "How are you?"

"Great, Ms. McCormick. How about you?"

"We're doing okay. You know, keeping busy."

Jinx resolutely continues to stare at her pizza, but then the worst happens.

"Sup, Jinxie." Then he *ruffles her hair in front of the girlfriend*.

Her face is on fire as she finally turns to look at him. "Hey."

"Ella," he addresses the girlfriend. "This is basically like my little sister."

"Oh, so this is the famous Jinx!" Ella gushes enthusiastically. "I've heard so much about you! What a cutie you are!"

Jinx would rather be anywhere than here. She would also rather be called just about anything other than "a cutie" right now. Normally, Blaine would pick up on this. But he's clearly so gaga over this Ella person that he doesn't notice.

Instead, he asks, "So what are you guys doing all the way over here?"

"Oh, just treating ourselves," says Aunt Helen. "It's been a hectic week for both of us."

"Cool, cool." He nods, clearly not taking in any of what she's saying. "Well, see you guys around."

"It was nice meeting you, Ms. McCormick," says Ella. "You, too, Jinx."

"Nice meeting you, too, Ella. I'm sure we'll see each other again soon."

Once they're gone, Aunt Helen looks at Jinx. "I would scold you for being so ridiculously rude, but . . . I think you've probably suffered enough already. Let's head home."

22

THE ARRIVAL

When they get home, Aunt Helen goes right to bed. That's okay with Jinx because she's not in the mood to be around other people. As soon as her aunt closes the door to her bedroom, Jinx begins resetting things. Ever since she and Ms. Simmons have talked about OCD, she's aware that what she's doing isn't "normal." Well, she always kind of knew that most people didn't do it. But now she knows it's an actual mental health disorder. You'd think that would make her want to stop. She tells herself that it should make her want to stop. But she doesn't stop. And you know what? She feels a little better after she's done. So there.

But now what does she do? She has to do *something*, because otherwise she's going to start thinking about Blaine and the fact that the *one person* she thought she could trust has turned out to have a secret girlfriend with crooked bangs. She can't decide which is worse, the girlfriend or that he kept her a secret. Why would he do that? And if he truly wanted to keep it a secret, why didn't it seem to bother him when she accidentally found out? None of it makes any sense and every time she thinks about it, her hands start groping for her camera. But if she takes a picture, the specter will be there. It'll be squatting in every image with its dark oily tendrils, spoiling everything, everything, everything.

Jinx wanders the house aimlessly for a little while. But it's a small house and it doesn't take long for her to reach her bedroom. She stands in front of her desk for a few moments before she realizes that she's staring at the camera obscura. It sits there like some innocent cardboard box, as though it wasn't able to project supernatural images.

She wants to look inside.

She also definitely does *not* want to look inside. The dark spirit is probably even closer now.

That means she should check, right? She reaches out her hand.

But then she hesitates. What if she looks inside and the specter is like *right in her face*?

Wait, shouldn't she want to know that? Maybe? But it's also the very *last* thing she wants to know. It's like biting her nails. She both wants to do it and doesn't want to do it. The push-pull of emotions is painful.

Finally she turns her back to the camera and heads downstairs. She grabs her skateboard, then pauses at the door.

Tappity-tappity. Tap. Tap. Tappity-tappity. Tap. Tap.

This time it works. This time she feels better. So she throws open the door and heads into the neighborhood.

She skates down to Buddy Attic Park. Once she gets there, she has to carry her board because the trail around the lake is gravel. The man-made lake is a weird, irregular shape, like a clawed hand with two fingers and a thumb. At one end, the two "fingers" are separated by a narrow peninsula, and at the very tip of that peninsula are a pair of benches where people can relax and enjoy the lake view.

Jinx sits on a bench and looks out at the water, which shimmers like gold in the late afternoon sun. It's not the kind of lake people swim in, but it does get stocked with fish to keep the algae under control, so people often fish on the other side. For some reason, though, hardly anyone comes to the little peninsula. It's always felt to Jinx like it was just for her and her dad.

Well, now just for her.

When Jinx was little, she and her dad would come out here sometimes, on days he was feeling up to it. He would bring his acoustic guitar, and she would bring her backpack filled with toys, or books, or a drawing pad with markers. He would strum classic rock tunes like "Where Is My Mind?" by the Pixies, and she would draw or whatever, humming along with him. Sometimes the frogs seemed to join in, singing with her father as if he was a goateed Disney princess. Other times, she'd spot a turtle on the bank and imagine it had come to hear her famous rock star dad jam out. If she was really lucky, there might be a blue heron, with its long legs and neck, or even a beaver from the dam up one of the "fingers" of the lake. The music would fill the air, the sun would sparkle on the water, and everything seemed pretty great. It was easy, in moments like that, to think they were happy.

But even then, she knew they weren't happy. Not really. Her dad spent a lot of time in bed. That was why Jinx would wander the neighborhood alone so much. It was probably the real reason everyone knew her so well. She was a talkative and inquisitive little girl with nothing to do and nowhere to go. If she's being honest, the free food actually came before she started taking pictures for people. Sometimes her dad couldn't get out of bed, and even when he could, he didn't always go shopping. They would go days without any food in the house. People seemed to pick up on that somehow and helped her out as much as they could. Later, when she taught herself how to take pictures, it was a way for her to pay people back, which made her feel a little better about it all.

Her father stayed in bed so much because he was so sad. Sad that Jinx's mom had died, sad that he had to quit being a rock star so he could raise Jinx. And sad that he had to leave Seattle and move back to his hometown so Aunt Helen could help him. He was probably also sad that Jinx wasn't very good at playing music. She didn't have the "ear" for it, he said. He bought the camera for himself as a hobby but lost interest in it pretty quick. So when Jinx asked if she could use it, he said sure. He told her it was good that she'd found a creative outlet, but she knew he wished that outlet had been music.

So Jinx's dad was sad for a lot of reasons, which is probably why he killed himself. Life just got too hard for him.

Now Jinx sits on a bench on the tiny peninsula and

watches the people walk along the lake path with their kids and their dogs. She watches birds come and go. She even spots a turtle nearby, sunning itself on a log. She hums "Where Is My Mind?" because she can't really remember any of the words besides "Where is my mind? Way out in the water, see it swimming."

Eventually the bugs get too annoying, and the sun begins to set, so she heads back home. Her aunt is still asleep. She was up really late for her, and she has the night off, so she'll probably sleep another couple of hours. Jinx can't decide if she would want the company or not. Not that she could do anything about it either way.

Jinx heads back up to her room, and there's that camera obscura, still lying on the desk. She sits in her chair and stares at it. What if it really is her father? He might be mad at her, but he wasn't usually an angry person, just a sad one. So why would he come? To forgive her for ruining his life? But what has she ever done to earn that forgiveness?

Then it hits her all at once. It's *so obvious* that she

literally smacks her forehead. It doesn't matter why he's coming or what he's planning to do. The important thing is that he's coming and she can finally say she's sorry. *That's* how she can earn his forgiveness! Back when he was alive, whenever she said she was sorry, he would always forgive her. So if she says she's sorry this time, and really means it—which she does—he'll forgive her again. Then maybe she'll stop thinking about it all the time. Then maybe she'll stop doing compulsive stuff like tapping on doorknobs. *Then* maybe she won't have to see Ms. Simmons twice a week for exposure therapy, which still sounds completely awful.

She picks up the camera obscura. Yes. That's what this *really* is. Not a cardboard box, or a camera, *or* a creepy spirit-channeling device.

It's a second chance.

Jinx walks over to the window. There isn't a whole lot of light left, but, hopefully, it's enough. She turns around and holds the camera obscura up to her eye.

There's the upside-down tree. But inside the camera obscura it looks different. Twisted, dry, desiccated. It looks dead.

And there's the specter. It's so close now that Jinx *should* be able to see details, but she still can't. It's like the spirit is concealed by a black fog or mist that undulates softly, warping the space around it. Just looking at it makes her stomach squirm. What does he look like? What if he looks dead? What if he still looks like he did when . . .

Jinx pulls the camera obscura away, her breath suddenly coming in heaves. She feels light-headed and like she might throw up. She drops to her hands and knees, hating the whimpering sounds in her gasps for air. Her eyes fix on the grains of the hardwood floor beneath her splayed hands. Her bandaged fingers scrape across it like she could dig her nails into it. She doesn't want to do this. She doesn't want to see.

"*Stop it*," she hisses to herself. "Don't be such a *baby*."

She reminds herself what Ms. Simmons said. That when

you finally face your fears, they're never as bad as you expect. Jinx just needs to be brave, that's all. Once her father gets here, even if he looks scary and gross, she'll apologize. Then everything will finally be okay. Really and truly okay.

Jinx steels herself for a moment, then stands back up. She holds the camera obscura in both hands, her expression set. She can do this. She has to do it.

She lifts the box to her eyes and peers once more at the dead, upside-down tree. The specter is so close now. It looks like it's floating just outside her window. Fear prickles up her spine but she still keeps looking. Her throat is dry, and a cold sweat breaks out on her forehead. She has to hold the camera obscura with both hands because they're beginning to shake. Her legs are so stiff that they're starting to hurt, but she can't sit down. She *won't* sit down. When he comes, she'll be ready for him. No matter what he looks like, she will tell him that she loves him and that she's sorry. And he'll say, *Thanks, Jinxie! Of course I forgive you!* Then he'll look like his old self and he'll pick up his guitar, which she has kept in her closet, completely free of dust. Maybe he'll notice that she's wearing one of his T-shirts and be like *Right on, Jinxie. That looks great on you!*

She grips the camera obscura as the dark specter completely fills her vision. Its murky tendrils feel like they're crawling along her arms, up her neck, reaching, reaching, reaching into her eyes, to fill her mind. Her heart is racing and she's terrified, but she is so, so *ready* to see her father again. *Here I am, Daddy! Here I am!*

But it's not her father.

The face becomes suddenly clear and it's . . .

Jinx?

But also *not* Jinx. This Jinx's eyes are totally black, like twin dark chambers. Purple veins spread out from the obsidian orbs like spiderwebs across her chalk-white face. Her smile is much too wide for a person, and her mouth is filled with long, needle-sharp teeth. Instead of colorful bandages, her fingers are tipped with curved black claws.

In a ragged and eager voice, this other Jinx says, "Hello, *me!*"

Jinx falls backward and smacks her head against the windowsill. The other Jinx looms over her, grinning maniacally. As pain pulses from the knot in her head, Jinx stares up in shock as she realizes that she's not holding the camera obscura anymore.

This specter—this other Jinx—is in the real world. But still the air around her ripples, dark and inky, like her very existence is a cancerous corruption of the world.

"Go away!" Jinx shouts stupidly, panicked, her head throbbing.

The other Jinx laughs almost hysterically, her veiny, pitch-black eyes wide with mirth. Then she lunges forward and grabs Jinx by the neck with both hands. Jinx tries to push her off, but between the knock on the head and the lack of air, she's too weak. She grabs a handful of hair and yanks as hard as she can, but all it does is make the other Jinx cackle gleefully and squeeze harder.

Jinx can't breathe. Her vision begins to swim and darken. She flails desperately, trying to grab at anything that might help her. But of course there's nothing around, because Jinx doesn't like clutter. Is this it? Is she going to die here, in her own bedroom, strangled to death by . . . herself?

But abruptly, the other Jinx releases her.

Jinx lies there, gasping, as the other Jinx straightens and looks down at her with a gloating expression. The space around her drips with raw malice. Every time she moves, streaks of darkness reverberate outward like ripples in a pond.

"W-Wha . . ." Jinx struggles to speak. She wants to ask who she is—*what* she is. But her throat hurts, and her voice is weak with terror and disgust.

The other Jinx's dark eyes fix on something above where Jinx is slumped against the floor. That's where Jinx's whiteboards are. The other Jinx leans across the desk and writes something, snickering to herself all the while. When she's finished, she climbs over Jinx, opens the window, and kicks out the screen. She straddles the windowsill, then pauses a moment to look back at Jinx and flashes her dark and dripping fanged smile.

"Later, Jinxie," she says in her ragged voice.

Then, even though they're on the second floor, she jumps.

It takes Jinx a couple of minutes before she's recovered enough to get to her feet. Her throat is sore and she's still a little dizzy, so she grips the windowsill as she looks out. There's no sign of the other Jinx.

Then she looks at her whiteboard. "Jinx's Day" has been smudged out. Over it, in a messy, uneven handwriting, has been written:

LUCKY'S NIGHT: FIX JINX'S LIFE
YOU'RE WELCOME 😁

23

THE ESCAPE

Blaine i really really need to talk to you

I should have told you about Ella, sorry!

Forget about that this is important. Can you meet me at the playground near my house?

Right now?

Yea rn

Long pause.

Jinx breathes a sigh of relief. She is on the verge of a total freak-out, but she's keeping it together because she knows she has to tell someone about this . . . entity calling herself Lucky. If Blaine had been too lost in girlfriendland to meet her, she wasn't sure who else would believe her.

Aunt Helen is downstairs, fumbling around the kitchen for breakfast. Jinx checks herself in the mirror, and just as she feared, bruises are already forming on her neck. If her aunt sees the bruises, there will be a lot of questions that Jinx doesn't know how to answer. So for now at least, she needs to hide them.

She yanks open her dresser drawer and rifles through clothes she hasn't worn in over a year, until she finds it. A lavender, sleeveless turtleneck that her aunt gave her for Christmas. At the time, Jinx had thanked her politely but secretly wondered how anyone could ever want a shirt that was too chilly for winter, but also too hot for summer. Well, she's grateful for it now.

Once she swaps out her oversize *Live Through This* T-shirt for the sleeveless turtleneck, it feels weirdly tight around her torso, but that's probably because she's been wearing nothing but men's XL shirts for so long. Another check in the mirror confirms that the bruises are now entirely hidden.

When she gets downstairs, she finds her aunt sitting at the table, eating from a cup of blueberry yogurt.

"Evening, kiddo." Aunt Helen waves her purple-coated spoon sleepily.

"Hey, Auntie."

Jinx wants to dash out of the house, but she can't let her aunt see how panicked she's feeling right now. So she forces herself to walk slowly, *calmly* to the door.

"Aw, you're wearing that shirt I gave you," says Aunt Helen.

"Yup." She reaches the door and leans against the frame so she can pull her shoes on.

"Isn't it a little late to be heading out?"

"Meeting Blaine." One shoe on.

"Oh?" Her aunt gives her a knowing smile. "Ready to forgive him?"

"I guess." The other shoe is on.

"How magnanimous of you. I'm counting on you to be home at a reasonable hour."

"I always am." She grasps the doorknob. "Later."

Tappity-tappity. Tap. Tap. Tappity-tappity. Tap. Tap.

Then she's out the door and jogging down to the court parking lot. But instead of heading to the street, she heads in the opposite direction to the tree line, and takes a narrow dirt path. She holds her hand up in case there are spiderwebs as she follows the unlit path through the trees until she reaches a clearing with a playground that has a small climbing structure, a slide, monkey bars, and a couple of swings.

She'd hoped to get there before Blaine. She kind of assumed she would, really, since he's always late for everything. And this time, it would have been nice to have a few minutes to calm herself before he showed up. But he's already waiting for her, drifting slowly back and forth on one of the swings. The playground isn't lit, and it's too dark to see his expression.

"Thanks for coming," she says.

"What's the emergency?" he asks.

Now that the moment has arrived to tell him, she isn't sure how to begin. This is why it would have been nice to have a moment before he got there to collect herself. Well, she'll just have to muddle through as best she can.

"So, uh, remember how I said there's nothing wrong with my camera?"

"Yep."

"But I wouldn't tell you how I knew that?"

"Sounds right."

"Okay, well . . ." She starts pacing back and forth. "I

know this sounds weird. Maybe even impossible, but I swear that the reason I knew was because the smudge wasn't just showing up on my dad's camera. It also showed up when I took pictures with my phone. It even showed up when I used that cardboard camera obscura."

"What does that even mean?"

"What I *thought* it meant was that I was like that spirit photographer guy who could channel the dead with cameras."

"Except he was a fake," he points out.

"I *know that*," she says testily. "And *obviously* I was wrong about that. But it turns out that I was channeling . . . something."

Jinx can't see his look of concern in the dark, but she hears it in his voice. "What do you mean 'something'?"

"It's like . . . I don't know, okay. I was looking into the camera obscura and she just—"

"She?"

"Yeah, I guess her name is Lucky? She looks like me,

199

kind of. But like a scary version of me. And then she started strangling me—"

"Hold up," interrupts Blaine, sounding more and more uneasy. "How could she strangle you if she was inside that camera thing?"

"That's what I'm trying to tell you." Jinx is struggling to keep her frustration in check. "She's loose! In the *real world*! She says she's going to 'fix' my life, but like, that's right after she almost *killed* me, so who even knows what that means!"

Blaine is silent for a moment, then shakes his head. "Sorry, I'm really trying here, but I still don't understand. What do you want me to do?"

"We have to stop her from rampaging around Greenbelt!"

Again he's silent. Then, "You want us to stop this . . . person . . . who looks just like you—"

"Except scary," clarifies Jinx.

"Right. Scary Jinx."

"Her name is Lucky."

"Sure. Lucky. And she's . . . like a supernatural creature?"

"You don't believe me," she says accusingly.

He holds up his hands. "I'm trying, honest! It's just *really hard* to accept that you have some . . . evil twin or something? For real?"

She groans in frustration. Then she turns on the flashlight app on her phone, pulls down her turtleneck, and shows him the bruises. "This is what she did to me before she took off."

With the light from her phone, she can finally see Blaine's expression. His eyes widen as he looks at her neck. "Jinx . . ."

"Bad, right?" she demands.

"Jinx . . ." He looks concerned, which is understandable. *She's* concerned, too. But he doesn't look angry that someone did this to her. He's giving her an altogether different kind of worried look. The not-good kind. "What did you do to yourself?"

"I didn't do anything!" Jinx turns off her phone light because she doesn't want to see that look anymore. "Well, okay, maybe I shouldn't have thought I could talk to my dad with a camera, but how was I supposed to know something like this could happen?"

He's quiet. Too quiet. Then he says, "Is your aunt home?"

"Huh? Why?"

His voice is gentle. Almost pleading. "Let's go see her."

Cold understanding dawns on her. "You think I hurt myself."

"Didn't you?"

"No! *She* did this to me!"

"Your . . . evil twin . . . Lucky?" His voice is heavy with doubt.

"Yes! I know it sounds crazy, but you have to believe me, Blaine. It really happened."

"I want to believe you. I really do. But you've had a rough couple of days, and then I see these horrible bruises on your neck, just like your Dad after—"

"This isn't like that!"

She didn't mean to shout it. All that does is freak him out more. She's only making things worse. He looks genuinely alarmed now but for all the wrong reasons.

"Let's go see your aunt. Please."

He reaches out to her.

She quickly steps back.

"Okay, then how about my place?" he asks. "My mom made too much food, as usual. You can have some leftovers and chill with us for a while."

"Blaine, I don't have time for that. Don't you see? She's out there somewhere. She could be hurting other people like she hurt me!"

"Seriously, Jinx." He stands and takes a step toward her.

She takes several steps back and starts glancing behind her, looking for the best escape route.

"If you take off, I'm going to call your aunt," he tells her.

Jinx hesitates. "But then she'll totally freak out, call up

everyone she knows in the neighborhood, and they'll all be looking for me."

"Yeah." He takes another step toward her. "Exactly."

She glares at him. "I didn't know if you were going to help, but I honestly didn't think you would actively try to stop me."

"What choice do I have?" She still can't see his expression in the gathering darkness, but his voice sounds pained. "I'm really worried about you."

"You *should* be worried," she tells him. "Just not about me."

He squares his shoulders and walks toward her with purpose. So she sprints back into the trees.

24

THE HACK

Jinx knows Blaine was serious about calling her aunt. She knows that while she's running through the trees, occasionally getting whacked in the face by branches, and once tripping over a root and almost breaking her neck, he's probably doing it right now. And that's a real problem. She'll have to dodge well-meaning but clueless neighbors while also searching for Lucky.

And what has Lucky been doing this whole time? Breaking things? Hurting people? Jinx thinks of those glittering obsidian eyes framed in spidery purple veins, of that too-wide mouth filled with rows of sharp teeth. She shudders. There's just no telling what Lucky is capable of, and nobody else knows that she even exists. It's all up to Jinx to stop bad things from happening.

She threads her way though the winding inner pathways of Old Greenbelt, which she probably knows better than anyone. But where should she look first? Lucky said she was going to "fix" Jinx's life, so she's probably going to places that Jinx goes all the time.

Roosevelt Center would be a good place to start, she decides. So she makes her way swiftly through the dark neighborhood, the squeak of bats and the occasional hoot of an owl filtering through the night air. She used to hate that the pathways are so poorly lit at night, but now she's grateful. As long as she can use these routes, nobody is going to find her.

But unlike the inner pathways, Roosevelt Center is brightly lit at night. Once she reaches the edge, she slows down. Part of her wants to just charge in, but she has to be smart about this. She can't get caught, or that's it. And once she finds Lucky, what will she do? What *can* she do against a supernatural creature like that? Well, one thing at a time. First, she has to locate her.

It's almost 9:00 p.m. Beijing Pearl and the co-op are already closed, and they seem fine. Joey's is still open and Jinx approaches cautiously. Ms. Lombardi is probably one of the people Aunt Helen would call first, so Jinx needs to make sure she's never in sight of the glowing restaurant windows. She gets just close enough to peak in. No Lucky. The movie theater is still lit up but looks okay, too.

Maybe Jinx was wrong? Or at least wrong about Roosevelt Center?

Next she checks the pool and the youth center, which are both closed and seem okay. The skate park is also Lucky free, but it is *not* people free. Blaine's friend Oscar is there, and he definitely seems like he's looking for someone. Maybe that isn't Jinx. She doesn't know him super well, after all. But if Blaine asked him to come all the way over from Hyattsville to help search, he would.

So Jinx skirts around the skate park and heads over to the community center and the library. The library is closed, but she forgot the community center doesn't close until 9:30 p.m. She comes around the corner and accidentally steps right into a giant pool of light. She glances around but doesn't see anyone.

She pauses for a moment, debating what to do next. Roosevelt Center is clear, at least for now. Should she find a good hiding spot around here and assume Lucky will show up eventually? Or should she search somewhere else?

She's still mulling that over when Bill emerges from the community center.

"Ms. Jinx?"

She could run, but he's not part of Aunt Helen's inner circle, so he probably doesn't know that people are looking for her yet. Monica might call him and ask him to help eventually, but not right away. On the other hand, if she runs, it'll definitely make him suspicious.

"Oh, hey, Bill," she says with what she hopes sounds like

a casual tone. "I didn't know you live around here."

"Nah, I'm still in College Park." He walks over to her. "But there's this lady here who teaches an amazing sewing class, and I've been wanting to up my game."

"Oh, cool. Well, have a good night." She turns to go.

"A little late for you to be out wandering alone," he says thoughtfully.

"I'm on my way home now," she assures him.

"It's pretty dark, you want a lift?"

"I'm good, thanks," she says, maybe a little too quickly.

His eyes narrow thoughtfully. "Hmm. Well, you be careful, Ms. Jinx."

"Thanks, I will."

She waves goodbye and forces herself to walk calmly to the nearby staircase that leads down to the library parking lot. Is he buying it, or is he right now texting his suspicions to Monica?

But if Jinx risks a look back, that might give her away, so she keeps her eyes forward and walks way slower down the stairs than she ever would normally. Then, when she reaches the bottom and is out of his line of sight, she sprints across the empty blacktop and into the woods.

Once she's safely hidden in the trees, she stops a moment to catch her breath and check her phone. She had turned the Do Not Disturb setting on so that she wouldn't be plagued by her aunt's frantic calls and texts. Sure enough, there are a bunch from her, Blaine, and Monica. There's also a weird notification from her social media app:

YOUR ACCOUNT HAS BEEN ACCESSED BY A NEW DEVICE. IF THIS IS NOT YOU, CONTACT OUR SECURITY TEAM IMMEDIATELY.

Of course it isn't Jinx. But what if Lucky knows everything that Jinx knows? Then she would know the password to her account.

"Oh no . . ." she whispers as she launches the app.

She checks her feed. Sure enough, there is a picture of

Swapna's house, festooned with toilet paper. The caption reads:

LMAO RICH PEOPLE SUCK

#SORRYNOTSORRY 😆

It's posted publicly for anyone to see. From Jinx's account. Everyone will think *she* did it.

She has to get over there now and tell Swapna and her mom what's really going on. She just hopes they believe her.

25

THE AMBUSH

Once more Jinx uses the inner pathways of Old Greenbelt to cross the neighborhood without being seen. But that plan only works until she gets to the edge of her neighborhood. Regular Greenbelt doesn't have the winding trails and dense wooded areas that have kept her hidden from her aunt, Blaine, and whoever else might be looking for her. She stops at the edge of a path and gazes nervously out at the open space before her. The wide lawns and spread-out houses look so exposed. Anyone will be able to see her . . .

Jinx shakes her head. Lucky has already shown that she isn't afraid to hurt people. She might attack the Kapoor family, too. Jinx needs to put their safety before anything else.

Even so, as she steps out onto the sidewalk, the hairs on the back of her neck rise. Some of the houses are dark, but others have glowing windows that feel like eyes watching her. She has to force herself to keep going, step-by-step, but not too fast, or she'll look even more suspicious than she already does—a twelve-year-old girl wandering alone at night.

After several nerve-racking minutes, she finally gets to Swapna's house. It looks even worse than in the picture. Strips of toilet paper hang from the roof, the portico, and the small tree on the front lawn. Three of the windows are smeared with . . . soap, maybe? And as she gets closer, she can see that the smears aren't random. A word is written in each one:

IS

SHE

WEIRD?

Is Lucky calling Swapna weird? Revenge for Swapna and the other girls at school calling Jinx a weirdo? Is that what Lucky meant by "fixing" her life? Jinx knows how much that word hurts, even though she's gotten used to pretending it doesn't. Still, this doesn't "fix" anything.

She stands there on the sidewalk, wrestling with indecision. Should she knock on the door? Try to explain to them what's happening? Surely they don't think Jinx could do something like this . . . right? What if they did? How would she prove it wasn't her?

"Jinx!"

Jinx turns to see Monica's head sticking out the passenger window of an approaching car. Seth is behind the wheel. They both look worried and upset.

"Wait, Jinx. Just stay where you are!" says Monica.

Jinx rocks back and forth on the balls of her feet as the car draws near. Should she explain, or run?

"Please, just get in the car," says Monica. "We'll figure this out together, I swear."

"I didn't do it!" says Jinx, walking backward down the sidewalk, away from the car.

"Seth, stop!" Monica snaps at him, and the car halts. Then she turns back to Jinx and reaches out her hand. "You're not in trouble. Just . . ."

The fear and heartbreak on Monica's face is so palpable that Jinx feels it like a punch to the chest. She's upset so many people. Maybe she should just—

"Janessa McCormick, *what is the meaning of this?*" thunders the voice of Ms. Kapoor. She's standing in the lit open doorway of her house in a pink robe and slippers. Her eyes are wide with fury as they move back and forth between Jinx and the toilet paper. Behind her stands Swapna in her pajamas, looking very shaken.

"It wasn't me!" says Jinx.

"I *saw* you!" shouts Swapna. "You were staring into my window, smiling up at me like some kind of *creeper!*"

"No! I swear that wasn't me! Please, you have to believe me!"

But neither Swapna nor her mother look like they're in a believing mood. And can she really blame them?

"Jinx, please just get in the car." Monica tries to calm everyone down. "Ms. Kapoor, I'm so sorry about this. Jinx is having a . . . well, an *episode* of some kind. I promise we'll work something out."

"I'm not having an—"

Jinx's phone buzzes again.

What's Lucky done now?

As she hurriedly pulls out her phone, she hears the sound of a car door opening. But she's too preoccupied with checking Lucky's latest update to process what that means.

The post is a photo of the front window of Joey's, now dark. Lucky's hand is spread wide, holding several eggs.

JOEY'S NEEDS A BREAKFAST MENU 🔍

"Why is she *doing* this?" Jinx yells.

She looks up from her phone and only then does she realize how close Monica is. Her ex-babysitter is reaching out with both hands to grab her.

Jinx stumbles back out of her reach, trips, falls, and catches herself on the sidewalk with her hand. Pain jolts up through her palm and into her wrist, but she immediately staggers back to her feet and sprints toward the safety and concealment of the inner pathways.

Monica might have grown up here, too, but nobody knows these trails like Jinx. She's probably making everything worse by running, but she has to stop Lucky. Right now, Lucky is acting like it's all funny jokes, and, thankfully, no one's been hurt yet. But she was *also* laughing hysterically while nearly choking Jinx to death . . .

So what else might she find "funny"?

26

THE CENTER

By the time Jinx gets back to Roosevelt Center, she's too late. Streaks of egg and bits of shell are stuck to the outside of Joey's.

"I'll clean it up, Ms. Lombardi, I swear . . ."

First, she has to find Lucky. But how? She's been consistently one step ahead. Like she's leading Jinx around by the nose. Is there any way to predict where she'll strike next? Is there a pattern of some kind? If there is, Jinx can't see it. First here, then there, then back here . . .

Jinx's blood chills as she realizes that Lucky *has* been leading her by the nose. She might have even *seen* Jinx looking for her at Roosevelt Center earlier and used Swapna's house to lure her away. Where else might she go that isn't *here*? Back to her house? Or maybe Blaine's house? Somewhere Jinx wouldn't want her to go.

Her phone buzzes again and she quickly opens the app. The latest post shows the front windows of the Beijing Pearl. This time Lucky's hand is holding a rock.

EGGS KEPT BREAKING SOOOOO 💥

"Wait, that's right around the corner!" A tiny bit of hope creeps into her voice. This time, she might catch her before she makes things worse.

But even as she lurches into a run, she hears the sound of breaking glass. It's already too late.

"No!"

She takes the corner so fast she almost trips again but manages to keep her feet under her. There's the Beijing Pearl, with a huge, ragged hole in the front window. Shards of glass lay scattered on the sidewalk, glittering sharply in the streetlight.

Jinx groans in frustration, but it's cut off by the sound of more breaking glass. She turns, and there is Lucky, standing beneath the GREENBELT movie theater sign. There's already broken bits of neon at her feet and she's holding another rock, ready to throw.

"Stop!" shouts Jinx as she sprints toward her.

Lucky grins at her, not even looking as she lobs the rock. Another crash, and a small rain of shattered neon as another letter disappears from the sign. She's apparently not been random in her throws, because she's only knocked out some of the letters. Now the sign spells:

REBEL

Lucky cackles like this is hilarious, then takes off. Jinx is already winded, but she pours on the steam, determined to catch her before she breaks anything else.

"Enough!"

Aunt Helen's strong hand grabs Jinx's upper arm.

"Let go! See? There she is!" Jinx pulls hard against her aunt's grip as she points. But Lucky is already gone. "I almost *had* her!"

"*I said enough!*" roars Aunt Helen. Her face is purple with fury, and the grip on Jinx's arm is strong enough to hurt. "What has gotten into you? How could you do all this!"

"I keep telling people, it's not me!" Jinx is trying to stay calm, but her arm hurts, her wrist hurts from when she fell, her head still hurts from before, and her pulse thunders in her ears. "It's not my fault! None of this is my fault!"

Aunt Helen looks like she's about to shout back, but she catches herself and visibly forces herself to take a moment. She loosens her grip a little so it doesn't hurt. Then in a much steadier voice, she says, "It's going to be okay, kiddo. I promise."

This was meant to make Jinx feel better. She knows that. But it doesn't make her feel better. It makes her mad.

"How can you *say* that?" Unshed tears sting her eyes as she struggles to get free. Her stomach seethes with anger and frustration and shame, like that boiling pot on the stove has been rattling this whole time and now, finally, it all spills out in one big gush of words. "How can you possibly say it's going to be okay? Why can't you understand that it's *never* going to be okay ever *again*!"

Aunt Helen stares at her as though she has no idea what to do or say. That makes sense because there is nothing she can do or say. But Jinx still has *plenty* to say.

"I'm so sick of people treating me like some fragile thing. Why would you even bother when it's so *obvious* that I'm *already broken*?"

Then Jinx's phone buzzes.

"Oh no, oh no, oh no!" she whimpers.

Aunt Helen is so stunned by Jinx's outburst, or maybe the full realization of just how messed up her niece truly is, that Jinx is able to yank her arm free. She takes off in the direction Lucky was heading as she fumbles for her phone.

This time the image shows the wide lawn in front of the library. The dense grass looks almost black in the dim lighting, so the large red gasoline canister really stands out. Lucky's hand holds a lit match.

ENOUGH FOOLING AROUND, TIME TO GET SERIOUS

A sharp pain lances through Jinx's side. She really isn't used to this much running. But she pushes through the pain and exhaustion as she sprints past a few restaurants and a law office. She's nearly there . . .

But she's still crossing the parking lot when she sees fire suddenly flare up. Too late. Again.

By the time she reaches the lawn, her side is cramping up so bad it's hard to breathe. The fire on the lawn has settled down to a moody flicker after the initial burst, and now she can see that once again it wasn't random. Lucky wrote a word across the lawn with the gasoline before she lit it on fire.

In giant flaming letters, the lawn says:

COMPLICIT

Jinx's phone buzzes again, but she's still staring at the fiery word, wondering what it means. Perhaps that no matter how she denies it, Jinx is complicit in Lucky's crimes? Is that fair? Does Jinx even believe in fairness?

Did she ever?

"Jinx . . ." Aunt Helen is staggering toward her, face flushed, breath wheezing. "Janessa . . ." Then she sees the fire and comes to a halt. She stares, mouth open, as the flames dance in her eyes. Then she turns to Jinx. "How *could* you?"

Maybe Jinx *is* complicit. Maybe if she'd done something different, Lucky wouldn't be here in the first place. But she can't go back and fix that. There are no do-overs. Jinx understood that the day her father died.

With a new, eerily calm resolve, Jinx checks her social

media account. The latest image shows Blaine's court. But not Blaine's house. Instead, Lucky is holding up the same gas canister as before, this time in front of Jinx's old house. The one she lived in with her father.

The caption reads:

WHERE IT ALL BEGAN AND WHERE IT ENDS

27
THE BEGINNING
AND THE END

Jinx was born in Seattle, but she was too young to remember that place because she and her dad moved to Greenbelt right after her mother died. Right after Jinx accidentally killed her. Her father had to quit his band because they toured a lot and he couldn't do that with a baby. The rest of the band split up soon after. In-Sufferable only made the one album, and there was only that one hit single.

At least the single made enough money for Jinx's dad to buy a house in Old Greenbelt, just down the street from his sister. It was similar to Aunt Helen's house, except it had a nice extension built onto the back where her father planned to set up a music studio.

But he never did set up that music studio. At first because he was so busy dealing with all the stuff that needs to happen when your spouse suddenly dies and didn't leave a will. Then later he didn't have time because he was a single parent with a baby. Even with Aunt Helen's help, babies take a lot of work. And by the time Jinx was old enough to go to school, and her father finally had some time to himself, he was just too sad to set up the music studio.

Things got worse after that.

By the time Jinx was eleven, he was often so drunk and high that he could barely stand. Jinx hated seeing him like that. Stupid and stumbling around, always looking like he was about to tip over, but somehow never doing so. It wasn't just the booze, Jinx knew. He also took marijuana and pills all the time. She'd learned about that stuff in health class, so she knew it was bad for him. But whenever she told him he should stop, he just . . . *laughed* at her. Like it was a great joke. Sometimes he would go on laughing for several minutes. He'd begin to trail off, but then he'd look at her somber face and start all over again. It made Jinx feel bad. She would stand there, her face and ears red with embarrassment while he continued to giggle and taunt her for her seriousness. But she didn't give up on him. Not ever. She loved her father more than anything, because when he was happy, he was the coolest, most amazing person in the world. He was fun and funny and the best musician who ever lived. He would make up songs about her right on the spot. Just grab his guitar and start singing silly stuff about how amazing she was. Jinx loved those moments. But as she got older, they happened less and less often.

On the day her father died—on the day he killed himself—he was completely wasted and in a lousy mood. She was not in a great mood either. It wasn't easy taking care of a dad who couldn't take care of himself. He'd thrown up on the kitchen floor but didn't clean it up.

Instead, he just went over to the couch and watched blankly as Jinx cleaned it up. She was so angry. She knew other kids didn't have to clean up their father's vomit. It wasn't fair. It wasn't right.

"Why do you have to be such a *loser?*" she asked scathingly.

He looked amused. "I'm a loser?"

"Yeah. Anyone who does drugs is a loser." That's what she had learned from a video in school.

Normally, this would be the moment when he would laugh at her. And he looked like he was about to. But then he stopped, and his expression became almost thoughtful.

"I guess the reason I'm a loser," he said mildly, "is because you ruined my life."

She stared at him, so hurt and furious she couldn't speak. The feelings were too big to come out in words. So she took her emotions out on the puddle of puke, scrubbing the kitchen floor with all her might. Until her arm ached and spots danced before her eyes.

By the time she looked up, her father had passed out on the couch. He probably wouldn't even remember what he'd said when he woke up. If only *she* could forget so easily.

She put away the cleaning supplies, then walked to the front door and pulled on her shoes. The house smelled bad, and no amount of air freshening was going to fix that right now. She needed to get out for a while.

But just before she left, she turned back and glared at her father's unconscious form slumped into the couch. The anger rose up again, hot and metallic on her tongue.

"I wish *you* had died instead of Mom," she hissed spitefully between clenched teeth.

She thought he was passed out. That he wouldn't hear what she said. But maybe he wasn't completely unconscious. Maybe, for once, he'd listened to her. Because when Jinx came home a few hours later, he'd hung himself.

When she entered the house, Jinx stopped, stared like she didn't understand what she was seeing. Like her brain couldn't make sense of it. Like it couldn't make sense of *anything* anymore. Something inside broke.

Blaine often came over to their house and never bothered to knock. Usually, it wasn't a big deal. But this time, he found Jinx slowly scrubbing her father's urine from the floor, her eyes glazed with shock. He tried to get her to move away from the body, but it was like she didn't even notice he was there.

Eventually, the EMS and police arrived. They took Jinx away on a stretcher. They took her father away in a body bag.

28

THE REAL TRUTH

Jinx hasn't seen her old house since that day. She's been to the court many times of course because that's where Blaine lives. But before, she always made a point of not looking in that direction. Now she has to look.

It appears mostly the same. Light gray vinyl siding and a red front door with a narrow wooden deck for the stoop. The new owners actually planted stuff in the little garden, and that's definitely an improvement over the neglected weed patch from Jinx's time there.

Thankfully, Lucky hasn't set the house on fire yet. Instead, she sits on the roof of the car that's parked out front. She's holding a lit match almost delicately between two curved claws, just watching it burn. Her black eyes flicker with the reflection of the flame. Her mouth is slightly open, so Jinx can just make out the jagged points of her fangs. The air around her still seems to darken and twist as though her very presence is a sickness, or a violation of nature. Maybe it is.

"Please don't set anything else on fire," Jinx says quietly.

Lucky looks up, her eyes widening in surprise. "Why not?"

"Because people live in that house."

"So what?" Lucky asks in her ragged voice. "What've they ever done for us?"

"That's not a reason to kill them."

Lucky appears to give that real thought, then shrugs. "Since they moved here after Dad died, they're probably the ones who deserve it the least."

"*Nobody* deserves to be burned to death."

Now Lucky grins, showing her needle-sharp teeth. "You

sure about that? After what they all did to us? Or I guess I should say what they *didn't* do?"

"What are you talking about?"

Lucky sighs, blowing out the match in the process. Then she slides down off the car. "I guess you're as dumb as you think you are. I even wrote it out on the lawn for you."

"You mean 'Complicit'?" asks Jinx. "I thought you wrote that because you're like my evil twin or whatever, so I'm as guilty of your crimes as you are."

"First of all, I'm not evil, just unfiltered," says Lucky. "Everything I say and do is something you have wanted to say or do but were too afraid."

"I would never burn down a house!"

"No," agreed Lucky. "Because you're too *scared*. But you *thought* about burning this house down. More than once. You see, Jinxie, I remember *everything*. Even the stuff you try to forget."

Jinx wants to tell her that she's wrong. That Jinx has never in her life thought about burning down this house. But what would be the point in lying now?

"Anyway, that's beside the point," Lucky says with a wave of one clawed hand. "When I wrote 'complicit,' I didn't mean you or me. I meant *everyone else*." She stretches out her arms. "The whoooole neighborhood knew what was going on here. They all knew Dad was an alcoholic and a drug addict. They knew he couldn't take care of us. And what did they do about it? Did they call the cops? Child services, maybe? Nah, they just gave us enough food that we wouldn't starve to death, and that was it." She looks up into the sky and shouts, *"Thanks a lot, Greenbelt! You really stepped up there!"*

"That's not fair!" says Jinx. "They helped us as much as they could, and they still do!"

Lucky nods agreeably. "Of course they do. To ease their own conscience. That look you always catch them giving you? It's not concern, or pity, or whatever else you'd like to pretend." Her jagged smile turns into a sneer and she walks slowly, deliberately toward Jinx. "What you see is *guilt*.

Because they should have done more, and they all know it."

"It's not that simple!" protests Jinx as she backs away. "They couldn't know for sure what was going on because *we* never told anyone. In fact, we covered it up as much as we could. If anything, it's our fault for hiding how bad it was."

"Our fault?" As Lucky gets closer, the air between them begins to shutter and warp. Her head tilts painfully to one side, too far, and her face contorts with fury. "*Our fault?* Next you're going to say it's our fault he killed himself."

"It *is* our fault!" Jinx's voice is shrill, and her eyes are once more stinging with unshed tears, but she can't help herself. These are things she's only ever felt deep down in the darkest parts of her heart, and Lucky is just *saying* them out loud—making *her* say them, like she's rubbing her face in it. "The last thing we told him while he was still alive was—"

"That we wished he died instead of Mom—yeah, yeah." Lucky is suddenly calm. Bored, even. She turns her back to Jinx and lights a match, gazing at it as she talks. "First, you're kidding yourself if you think he ever cared about what we had to say. Also, we are a child, he was a freaking adult. Lastly, we were absolutely right. He *was* a loser, and we *would* have been better off with Mom. Heck, we would have been better if we'd moved in with Aunt Helen when we first got here. At least somebody would have been paying attention."

There is so much Jinx wants to say. That Lucky's wrong? That she's being *unfair*? She's about to shout back at her. Tell her she's a mean bully who only . . .

Then she notices that Lucky is still holding the match. Even though the fire is now *burning* her finger and thumb. Lucky stares at it, still grinning her fanged grin. But her black, venous eyes are wide, she's blinking rapidly, and her jaw is clenched. Lucky might be some supernatural creature, but the fire is still clearly causing her pain.

"Stop hurting yourself!"

Lucky's lip curls into a snarl as she tosses the match. "What do you care? I'm the part of you that you don't like, right? The part that you *strangle* every chance you get."

Then she lights another match and this time holds her hand directly over it. The flame licks her palm as she gives Jinx a fixed grin, her lip twitching and nostrils flared because she is clearly in pain.

"Please . . . stop . . ." begs Jinx.

But Lucky doesn't. Her smile has turned into a wide grimace of agony, and the stench of burning flesh permeates the air. But still she doesn't move her hand away from the flame.

"Sorry," Lucky says through clenched fangs. "I guess suffering is all I got left."

"*No!*" Jinx lunges forward and grabs her wrists, forcing them apart and making her drop the match. "You have me!"

Lucky's face twists in fury. "You *hate* me!"

"I don't hate you!" Jinx grips Lucky's wrists as she tries desperately to find words that won't come. "I just . . . I don't . . ."

Lucky watches her struggle for a moment, then gives her a look of disgust. "Yeah, that's what I thought."

Then she slams her forehead into Jinx's.

They both stagger from the explosion of pain. Stars swim through Jinx's vision, but she still holds on to Lucky's wrists.

"*I'm just scared of you, okay?*" she shouts directly into Lucky's face. "You got all the anger, and I got all the fear! You were big and strong and out of control! I was afraid that we would hurt someone, so I guess I *did* strangle you. But I'm sorry! I'm so, so sorry!"

A welter of emotions pass across Lucky's face. Resentment, confusion, distrust.

"Yeah?"

"Yeah," Jinx says firmly. "And you know I can't lie to you. Because you're me."

Finally, a tiny hint of hope glimmers in Lucky's void-like eyes, like starlight in the night sky. Then she slowly begins to droop, sinking to her knees.

Jinx follows her down, still holding her hands, so that they kneel facing each other.

"I just . . ." Lucky's ragged voice shakes with a vulnerability that Jinx hasn't heard before. "I'm here, too, you know. I don't actually go away just because you want me to."

"I get it now." Jinx gently presses her bruised forehead to Lucky's. "You're a part of me. I can't shut you out. And I don't want to anymore. You're the strong one, after all. So I guess I . . . I *need* you if we're actually going to get through this. And maybe I actually want to now. For both of us."

Their foreheads are still touching, so all Jinx can see of Lucky's face are her dark, star-filled eyes. But she can hear the smile returning to Lucky's voice.

"Yeah, you *do* need me. And we *will* get through this. I promise."

Now Jinx is smiling. "How about no more burning stuff, though, okay?"

"Ugh, fine. You know, I didn't used to be this bad. But

because you locked me up all the time, I got worse. So from now on, sometimes you gotta let me do my thing."

"I will," Jinx promises.

"And I guess . . . sorry about . . . all the stuff."

"Me too."

Jinx closes her eyes, and the tears that had been building up the whole night finally fall down her cheeks. And they feel good. Warm and soothing. For the first time in a very long time, Jinx feels whole. It radiates outward, thoughtful and caring but also strong and ferocious. How could she ever have wanted to shut away this amazing part of herself? It was like she'd been trying to cope with her grief and loss while she had one hand tied behind her back. No wonder she was so miserable.

Sometimes, when you face your fear, when you open that door, you discover that something *is* there after all. It can be cruelty, or ignorance, or indifference.

Or sometimes, it's you.

29

THE LUCKY ONE

"Jinx! Oh, man, Jinx!"

Jinx realizes that she's alone now, kneeling in the middle of the court with her forehead pressed to the blacktop. Blaine's voice sounds at once worried and relieved. She hears his sneakers slap loudly on the blacktop as he comes closer. Then she feels his hand on her shoulder.

"Jinxie, you okay?"

She looks up at him. Her forehead is bruised. Her face is smeared with grime except for the twin tear tracks that run down her cheeks. And she smiles.

"You know what? I think I might actually be getting there."

Blaine looks like he wants to believe her but isn't sure he should. "You're not going to split again? Even if I text your aunt that I found you?"

She shakes her head.

He lets out a relieved sigh and plops down next to her on the blacktop. He takes out his phone and sends the text. After that's done, he gives her a tired smile. "You really ran us ragged there for a while."

"I didn't mean to," she says.

"I know." He reaches over and ruffles his hair.

Jinx still hates when he does that, and she can feel Lucky rumbling around inside, wanting to poke back at him somehow. Well, she did promise to let her do her thing sometimes . . .

So she says, "Your girlfriend has a terrible haircut."

Blaine stares at her in surprise. Probably because she hasn't said anything that salty in about a year. Not since before her dad died. Then he laughs. "Yeah, she kinda does. I think she's convinced it looks edgy or something?"

"It just looks dumb," says Jinx.

"Well," says Blaine, "she also has some *positive* qualities."

"Like what?"

"Like she thinks you're super cool."

"Hmph." But Jinx can't quite stop herself from smiling a little. "I *guess* I'll give her a chance, then."

"Thank you," he says sincerely. Then he reaches over like he's going to ruffle her hair *again*.

But she ducks her head away and glares at him. "The next time you do that, I'm going to bite your hand."

He winces. "I guess you're getting a little old for it, huh?"

"Uh, yeah."

He smiles sheepishly. "Sorry."

"Forgiven."

They sit there on the blacktop in silence for a little

while. Jinx is surprised to see that the night sky has shifted into a warm pink predawn light. None of them have slept the whole night. As if that realization opens a floodgate, she feels a new wave of tiredness. After a moment of hesitation, she lets her head lean into Blaine's shoulder, and he doesn't push her away.

Finally, Aunt Helen appears, face red, huffing and puffing. She runs toward them.

"Oh boy . . ." Jinx stands and brushes off her bottom. "Time to face the music."

"Good luck," murmurs Blaine.

She gives a wan smile, then turns to her aunt.

"Hey, Auntie." She braces for the shouting.

But instead, her aunt continues to charge forward until she scoops her into a giant bear hug.

"Oh, kiddo, thank goodness you're okay." Aunt Helen squeezes her fiercely. Neither of them are huggers, so they stand there in awkward embrace for entirely too long. But Jinx for once finds she doesn't mind at all.

At last her aunt releases her. Her eyes squint as she takes in the bruise on Jinx's forehead.

"We'll get some ice for that," she mutters.

"Thanks," says Jinx.

They stand there and look at each other.

Then Jinx says, "I got a lot of stuff to make up for."

"Yeah," agrees Aunt Helen. "You do."

After some much-needed sleep, Jinx gets to work. She helps clean up the egg mess at Joey's, and the toilet paper at Swapna's house. She doesn't have the money to replace the window at Beijing Pearl, the sign in front of the movie theater, or the grass on the lawn in front of the library, but Monica and her friends offer to do a special fundraiser cosplay photo shoot. And apparently, people are willing to pay money for exclusive *Battle Maidens* cosplay pictures. A *lot* of money, in fact. Enough to pay for everything *and* the materials that Bill needed to make the costumes.

All that is pretty easy. The hard part is apologizing.

Jinx knows that trying to convince people it was all Lucky's fault would be impossible. And more important, would it even be right to blame Lucky? After all, Jinx decided to accept that part of herself. She *promised* that she would. Not just the good bits, but all of it. Starting with this.

So she *wants* to apologize. But . . .

"I don't know what I should say," she tells her aunt as they walk the inner pathways to Roosevelt Center, where Jinx will begin her apology tour.

Aunt Helen thinks about it for a second. "Well, first of all, are you actually sorry?"

"Of course."

"You feel bad?"

"Yeah."

"Why do you feel bad?"

That brings Jinx up short. It just seems so obvious. "Well, I mean, these people have always been so nice to me."

"Maybe you start there, then. Not with guilt but with

telling each of them how much they mean to you. How much you *appreciate* them. I think the rest will come from there."

That does sound a little less daunting. "Okay, I'll try that. Thanks, Auntie."

"That's what I'm here for, kiddo."

"And I guess I should start with you."

"With me?" Her aunt looks surprised.

"Because you *are* always here for me. Like, always."

Her aunt smiles and blinks rapidly. "Thanks. That . . . means a lot to me. I'll be honest, all of this . . . losing your dad, suddenly becoming a full-time single parent . . . it hasn't been easy."

"Oh, I knew that," admits Jinx.

Aunt Helen looks surprised. "You knew?"

"Yeah, you tried your best, but you're not actually that great at hiding it."

Her aunt looks crestfallen, and Jinx winces.

"Sorry, Auntie. You know, Blaine told me that

sometimes I'm like a black hole. Things go in, nothing comes out. But from now on, I'm going to try my hardest to be here for you, too."

"Thanks, kiddo," says her aunt. "And I promise, things will get easier. We're a team, and if we work together, we can handle anything life throws at us."

That makes Jinx feel even more reassured. When they reach Roosevelt Center, Jinx apologizes to them each in turn: Ms. Lombardi, Mr. Lo, Ms. Linkenholker, and Mr. Humphries. She tells them how grateful she is to have them in her life. How much she appreciates everything they've given to her. Not just the food, but the help and the encouragement. As she's talking, she can feel Lucky rumbling around inside: *If these people are so great, why didn't they call child protective services? Why didn't they do something to help us when we* really *needed it?*

Maybe they should have, or maybe not. But Jinx decides that if she wants to be forgiven, she needs to *do* some forgiving as well. So she lets that resentment go.

They all tell her how much they appreciate her words, and that they understand she's had a really tough year, and of course they forgive her. Adults are easy that way. Maybe because they've had more time to make their own mistakes and understand how hard it is sometimes to know what the right thing to do is. But the last stop on her apology tour probably won't be so easy. In fact, it takes several days before Swapna even agrees to see her.

Her aunt has to work that night, so Blaine walks down with her to the Kapoor house. Since she's already on a roll, she decides to hit him with an apology on the way.

"Sorry I got jealous of Ella. Now that I've had a chance to hang out with her, she's actually pretty cool, I guess."

"Well, I handled it in the worst way possible," admits Blaine. "I shouldn't have kept something like that from you."

"True."

They walk a little farther, and then she says something that she hasn't even thought about before, but as soon as she says it, she knows it's true.

"You saw the same thing as me, and I never asked you if you were okay."

He doesn't respond right away, but she knows that he knows she's talking about seeing her dad's body. So she waits.

Finally, he says, "Yeah."

"I'm sorry I never realized that before."

His face tenses up, then he nods. "Thanks."

"I don't know what I'd do without you," she tells him.

After a moment, he surprises her by saying, "Same."

She doesn't really know why he'd say that, but asking him would feel like she was fishing for compliments, which would be gross. So she decides to leave it at that for now. Maybe she should simply trust that it's true, even if she doesn't understand it?

Once they reach the Kapoor house, Jinx's stomach begins to squirm with nerves. Not only did Lucky mess up their house, but she made it personal with that IS SHE WEIRD? message. And if Swapna really had seen her being all creepy out on the lawn, that would have been extremely scary.

Besides, kids aren't nearly as forgiving as adults.

Ms. Kapoor answers the door. Jinx thanks her for always being so supportive and also for the delicious food. Swapna's mom seems a little thrown off by this approach, but understanding dawns when Jinx then moves into the apology.

After she's finished, Ms. Kapoor says, "Thank you, Janessa. I know that you haven't had an easy life, and I appreciate that you refuse to let yourself be defined by that. As long as you don't give up on yourself, I won't give up on you."

She calls Swapna down and they wait in awkward silence as they listen to her footfalls on the stairs.

When Swapna appears, she looks really nervous.

"Hey," says Jinx.

"Hey," says Swapna.

"I'm really sorry for everything I did, especially for scaring you like that. You've always been nice to me, even though you're super popular and I'm a big weirdo. But then—"

"I shouldn't have called you a weirdo," Swapna interrupts.

Jinx isn't here to get into an argument, but that is just a silly thing to say. "It's fine. Everybody at school thinks I'm weird. That's why they avoid me."

"No, they're all just intimidated because you're so cool and mature."

"*Mature?*" Jinx has no idea what she's even talking about.

"I was intimidated, too. But after everything that's happened, my mom and I talked about some of the stuff you've had to deal with. I didn't really understand that you never got to be a kid like me. When I started thinking about it like that, I realized that I wasn't very nice to you, even though you always tried to be nice to me."

"I was nice?" Jinx has lost the whole thread of this conversation.

"You did all that work on my headshots and didn't even ask for money."

"And also?" prompts Ms. Kapoor.

Swapna's cheeks redden. "I used the headshots for my latest commercial audition and, uh, I got the job."

"You *what*?"

"Yeah, I'm officially a clothing model now, and I'm pretty sure some of that was thanks to you. Not just because of the headshot, too. You also took the time to coach me on how to be more relaxed in front of the camera."

Jinx grins sheepishly. "You picked up on that, huh?"

"Not until I went to this other shoot," admits Swapna. "I was like 'Why am I way more tense than I was for my headshots? Wait, is this what I'm *normally* like?' So then I tried to remember all the stuff you did to distract me and how that felt, and it was way easier to relax."

"Huh." Jinx hadn't meant to teach Swapna any-thing. She'd just been trying to put her subject at ease, like any good photographer should. "Well, I'm glad it worked out."

"Me too," says Swapna. "And I promise that this school year, I'm going to make sure you aren't alone all the time."

"Oh," says Jinx, taken by surprise. "Thanks."

She is still pondering all this as she and Blaine walk home. She has to admit, it would be nice to have some friends her own age.

"Pretty cool that Swapna's a professional model now," says Blaine.

"Yeah," agrees Jinx.

"Hey, maybe we *should* call you Lucky."

Jinx's eyes go wide.

He holds up his hands. "Kidding, kidding . . ."

"Jinx is an ironic nickname anyway," she says loftily.

He grins. "Oh, excuse me."

After that, things start to get better for Jinx. But she still goes to see Ms. Simmons twice a week. She has a way to go before she gets her OCD under control and deals with her father's death. Grief can take a long time to run its course. How long?

As long as it takes.

And now, she thinks that she—*all of her*—is worth the effort.

A NOTE FROM THE AUTHOR

Hello, dear readers. The characters in this book are fictional, but obsessive-compulsive disorder is very real. I learned about it from some friends of mine who have had OCD since they were kids. They learned to manage it as they got older and now it's just a part of themselves that they love as much as any other part. I'm pretty confident that Jinx would get there, too!

I did a lot of research about OCD, of course, and spoke to a licensed therapist about it. Everything that Ms. Simmons says in the book about OCD is true. If you'd like to learn more about it, you can visit the International OCD Foundation at kids.iocdf.org.

Something else that Jinx deals with in this book is child abuse. Her dad didn't hurt her directly, but he also didn't take care of her. That's called neglect, and it is a form of abuse. If you or someone you know is suffering from child abuse, you can call/text 1-800-422-4453 or go to childhelphotline.org.

And one more very important thing: If you are having thoughts of suicide or self-harm, please call/text 988 or chat with someone online at 988lifeline.org.

I had a lot of help with writing this book. In particular, a huge thanks to Ryan Benyi, Stephanie Perkins, and Gini Kelley for their knowledge, enthusiasm, and time. Thanks to Greenbelt Homes Inc., aka Old Greenbelt, where this novel is set, and apologies for the liberties I took with names and geography in service to the narrative. Thanks also to my editors, Zack Clark and Anjali Bisaria, and my agent, Jill Grinberg, and her whole team at JGLM for everything they do to keep me sane! Last, as always, thanks to Logan and Zain, who are both off on their own adventures in college now but are still a huge source of support and inspiration for me.

ABOUT THE AUTHOR

KELLEY SKOVRON is the author of *The Hacker's Key, The Ghost of Drowned Meadow,* and the GI Joe Classified series for kids, as well as books for teens and adults. She and her cat live in a bread factory in Ohio now, but they used to live in Greenbelt, which is why she knows it so well! Learn more about Kelley's books at kelleyskovron.com.